The Box of Cards

A New Sherlock Holmes Mystery

Note to Readers:

Your enjoyment of this new Sherlock Holmes mystery will be enhanced by re-reading the original story that inspired this one –

The Adventure of the Cardboard Box.

It has been appended and may be found in the back portion of this book.

A NEW SHERLOCK HOLMES MYSTERY

THE BOX OF CARDS

THE FOOL.

JUDGEMENT.

CRAIG STEPHEN COPLAND

The Box of Cards

A New Sherlock Holmes Mystery

16

Craig Stephen Copland

Published by:

Conservative Growth Inc.
3104 30th Avenue, Suite 427
Vernon, British Columbia, Canada
V1T 9M9

Cover design by Rita Toews.

ISBN: 1530208130

ISBN 13:   978-1530208135

Dedication

To The Bootmakers of Toronto – The Sherlock Holmes Society of Canada. Since 1972, the Bootmakers of Toronto have been the leading Canadian society for the appreciation and enjoyment of Sherlock Holmes. My membership in this splendid organization of friendly, encouraging, eccentric, and quirky Sherlockians led to my quest of writing a new mystery, inspired by each of the stories in the original Canon. I am deeply grateful.

Welcome to New Sherlock Holmes Mysteries –

"The best-selling series of new Sherlock Holmes stories. All faithful to The Canon."

Each story is a tribute to one of the sixty original stories about the world's most famous detective. If you are encountering these new stories for the first time, start with *Studying Scarlet,* and keep going. (https://www.amazon.com/dp/B07CW3C9YZ)

If you subscribe to Kindle Unlimited, then you can 'borrow for free' every one of the books.

They are all available as ebooks, paperbacks, hardcovers, and in large print.

Check them out at www.SherlockHolmesMysteries.com.

NEW SHERLOCK HOLMES MYSTERIES

WWW.SHERLOCKHOLMESMYSTERY.COM

Contents

Acknowledgments

Like all writers of Sherlock Holmes fan fiction, I owe a debt to Arthur Conan Doyle. Or, if you are a true Sherlockian, to Dr. John Watson who recorded the brilliant exploits of the world's most famous detective. This particular story is a tribute to the original story, *The Cardboard Box,* and borrows liberally from the plot, character, vocabulary, and even entire sentences.

A special thanks is given to Mr. Dennis Martin of Pinehurst, North Carolina, an enthusiastic reader of *New Sherlock Holmes Mysteries*. He made some delightful and creative suggestions for this story and they have been duly included.

The illustrated tarot cards are from the 1909 Rider Waite edition, illustrated by Pamela Coleman Smith.

As in previous books in this series, I gratefully acknowledge my debt to my high school English teachers and university professors who encouraged a love of reading and writing, and instructed me in the basics of grammar and composition. And again, I acknowledge the dear friends and family who continue to encourage me in this pleasant if quixotic quest of writing a new mystery to correspond to every story in the original Canon.

Chapter One

Sherlock Holmes Reads My Mind

THE MAGICIAN.

Not all of the cases about which I have written required Sherlock Holmes to use his peculiar capacity for synthetic reasoning and his remarkable mental qualities in identifying and apprehending a man, or occasionally a woman, who had committed, or was about to commit, a murder. But many of them did.

Not all of the cases I have selected involved London's only consulting detective in using the process of scientific deduction to ascertain who had robbed, by means of theft or blackmail, his or her fellow citizen of funds, jewelry, property, or inheritance. But many of them did.

And not all of the adventures in which I accompanied him, as the chronicler of his accomplishments, exposed those unbridled passions of the human heart which lead to acts of vile revenge, rages of jealousy, or plots and machinations designed to do devastating emotional injury to a victim. But many of them did.

Yet there has only been one to date that intertwined in the darkest and most terrible chain of events all of the above: impending murder, blackmail, revenge, hatred, cruelty, and the irresistible compulsions tied to feelings of betrayal, burning desires for intimacy, and the breaking of the bonds of marriage.

It is to this case that I now set my pen.

Some poets lament the coming of April, what with its miserable cold, everlasting rain, and ceaseless damp breezes, claiming it to be the cruelest month. They are entirely off the mark. August is the cruelest month. By August, the lovely lilacs of early summer have withered and fallen back into the dead ground. The desires and memories of spring have faded. The dull rains that brought life to the dormant roots of winter have passed. By August, all we are left with is the relentless heat of the sun, without so much as a cool breath of breeze, let alone a gust of wind.

Thus it was in mid-August, in the year of Our Lord, 1905. With the thermometer above ninety, some wags, trying to affect the swagger of Americans, announced that it was "hot enough to fry an egg on the sidewalk." Holmes dismissed such claims with utter disdain, noting first that England did not have sidewalks, we had pavements; and second, that were such pavement sufficiently hot, it would melt the bottoms of our Wellingtons. And, of course, it would be a stupid waste of a good egg.

I endured the blazing heat. I had learned to tolerate it during my service under the Raj. It was a small price to pay to have successfully begged off accompanying my wife on a visit to her relatives in Blackpool, under the guise of having to assist my friend, the unique and exceptional Sherlock Holmes, in his pursuit of the criminals who never ceased to be active in the heart of the Empire, this teeming city of five millions of people.

On the particular afternoon in which this story begins, however, there was no criminal case in Holmes's docket. I had fallen into a bit of a brown study while absorbing the entire *Daily Chronicle,* and Holmes was reading through the day's mail. The paper's front page announced the appointment of the American president, Theodore Roosevelt, to mediate a peace treaty between Japan and Russia. Over the past few years, to my mind, the Japanese had become highly expansive, seizing land and territories that did not belong to them. A few years back, they went to war with China and ended up taking control of a piece of Manchuria and all of the island of Formosa. Last fall, they had blockaded then occupied Port Arthur, on the east coast of Asia. The Czar had been outraged and sent his Baltic Fleet all the way from St. Petersburg, around the Cape, and into the waters of the China Sea to do battle with the fleet of Nippon. The Russians had been soundly defeated, annihilated in fact, by the Japanese, and now the victors were exacting a punishing peace. I was not a fan of the growing Asian power and made a passing comment to that effect.

"And why," queried Holmes, without looking up, "do you find their actions so objectionable?"

"Good heavens," I responded indignantly, "a nation cannot just seize and claim a part of another country. That cannot be permitted."

"Oh, really," said Holmes, his voice tinged with his habitual imperiousness. "Is that not exactly what we British have done for the past three hundred years? As have the French, the Belgians, the Dutch and, even farther back, the Portuguese and the Spanish?"

"That is not at all the same," I countered. "We brought European civilization to primitive peoples. When did we ever take whole territories away from advanced nations?"

"We could start with Canada. I do believe that the French would consider themselves to be advanced Europeans even if we do not. And I rather suspect that the rulers of India believe that they were every bit as civilized before the imposition of the Raj as afterward. I do not think that the Japanese thought terribly highly of Admiral Perry blowing up their harbor, nor the Chinese of our doping them with opium. The Belgians have hardly played the role of gentlemen in their Congo. Neither did we in taking the Cape away from the Afrikaans. Shall I continue?"

I had to ruminate about that for a minute or two.

"If your observation is correct," I countered, "then why is it that all of Europe now objects to the expansion of the power of their Land of the Rising Sun, or whatever it is they call themselves?"

"Only because they came late to the game," sniffed Holmes. "They are now copying Europe and doing exactly what we did. They are only condemned because they are doing so two centuries too late."

I was not in the mood to argue the point, so I let it pass, said nothing, and returned to other stories in the newspaper. A few minutes later, I tossed it aside and rose to prepare a cup of tea.

"They are *not* just sowing their wild oats," said Holmes.

"Of course they are," I replied, without thinking. Then I turned to him, stunned. "Just how, in heaven's name, Holmes, did you know what I was thinking? Really, there are times when you truly are possessed by another power."

He laughed, merrily, but warmly. "Oh, my dear Watson. There was nothing occult about what just happened. I was in rapport with you while you were reading the third page of the newspaper, in which the story of the disappearance of the Cushing children is recorded. The writer noted, did he not, that there is some debate as to whether or not foul play was involved. Some have speculated that these two young people, having had the normal pleasures of youth so removed from them by their religiously fanatical parents, might just have run off in order to have a good time at the beaches along with all of their peers. That is the story you were reading, was it not?"

Indeed, it was.

"And as you were reading it, at you first scowled and shook your head when you considered the speculations of nefarious acts by criminal elements, and then upon finishing the last paragraph, your glance went to the mounted photograph on the bookshelf. I refer to the framed one of you as a handsome young man, resplendent in your uniform of the Northumberland Fusiliers, and as you recalled fondly the joyful, irresistible pleasures of youth your hand stole toward your old wound. Your vacant expression said that you imagined that these two young people were doing no more than escaping the suffocating bonds of their parents and reveling in the freedom of their age. Am I correct?"

He was; he always was.

"And," he continued, "having remembered your own youth so fondly, you transferred to them the same motives and feelings and wonderful foolishness that is the birthright of those who are yet to reach the age of twenty."

"I did," I acknowledged. "And for that reason, I am convinced that all this talk of kidnapping, without a shred of evidence, is poppycock and scaremongering."

"And you are wrong."

His saying this offended me since, as far as I could see, there was nothing to indicate any other conclusion than the one I had reached.

"And just how, Mr. Sherlock Holmes," I snapped, "do you know that?"

He laughed, again in a friendly if infuriating manner.

"I am sorry, my dear friend. That was not fair of me, was it? I know you to be wrong because of the note that I am holding in my hand and just finished reading a moment before you put down the newspaper. Here, have a read."

He did not get up off the sofa but merely stretched out his long arm, offering the letter with the expectation that I would come over and fetch it. Grudgingly, I did as he expected. The note was from Inspector Lestrade, and it ran:

Holmes. Concerning the Cushing children. The situation has become beyond strange and therefore appropriate to such skills as you possess. Meet me at the Paxtons Head in Knightsbridge at 4:00 pm. Lestrade.

"Might I prevail upon you," asked Holmes, "to join me. I do promise to behave myself and not disabuse you of any more of your befuddled notions."

I harrumphed but agreed all the same. He knew, and so did I, that there was nothing that so stirred my blood as helping Sherlock Holmes in his brilliant pursuit of evil-doers. Of course, I would go with him. It was already approaching 3:15 pm, but I would have time to fix and enjoy my tea before we departed 221B Baker Street and made our way in the afternoon swelter to Knightsbridge.

At twenty minutes before four o'clock, we hailed a cab on Baker Street and proceeded south, across Oxford Street, and along Park Lane. As we rattled down the avenues, I chanced to remark on Holmes's "mind-reading" ability.

"You know, Holmes, I have concluded that the skill you possess in discerning what is going on inside a man's head must be a necessary attribute of consulting detectives. Did not Mr. Auguste Dupin exhibit similar abilities? Remember when he reasoned from Chantilly to Orion, to Dr. Nichols, to Epicurus, and then on back to Stereotomy, the street stones and finally beginning with fruitier. The same as you do. Quite alike in that regard, the two of you."

Sherlock Holmes visibly stiffened and glared at me with a look of having been insulted and offended.

"Good Lord, Dr. Watson. Are you incapable of using your brain to do any more than fill the void inside your cranium? That Dupin fellow is nothing but a complete work of fiction. Edgar Allen Poe concocted him entirely out of whole cloth. Anyone who is not resident in Bed'lam can see that."

I was taken aback but was not about to let the insult pass without a rebuttal.

"I beg to inform you, Holmes, that there are thousands of readers of Mr. Poe's accounts throughout the English-speaking world who do believe the stories to be factual, and we are *not* all destined to be admitted to Bethlehem."

His face softened, and his tone changed to one, equally annoying, of familiar condescension. "Really, my friend, it is utterly beyond the realm of human reason. Does anyone with intelligence above that of a moron believe that there could ever have existed an enormous orangutan that would engage in shaving his bearded face, and upon being discovered, become a razor-wielding monster who decapitated an elderly woman, murdered her daughter, stuffed the daughter's body up the chimney feet first, and whose voice was identified by a French gendarme as a Spanish speaker, by the silversmith as an Italian, by a Dutchman as French, by an Englishman as a German, by a Spaniard as English, and by an Italian as a Russian. Honestly, Watson, could there be anything more absurd?"

I suppose he was right on that score. I could imagine people mistaking a language for one other than their own, but the existence of an ill-tempered, murderous ape was a bit too much of a stretch. I let that matter drop as well.

Chapter Two

Horror in Knightsbridge

THE HIGH PRIESTESS

We continued on past the Duke of Wellington's modest cottage and then turned right and rumbled the few blocks to Paxtons Head. Inspector Lestrade, as wiry, as dapper, and as ferret-like as ever, was waiting for us inside. Without rising from his seat, he gestured to two chairs on the opposite side of his table.

"Have a seat. If you are hungry, I can recommend the fish and chips. They have been serving some version of that dish on this site for the past two hundred years and have finally managed to get it right. I did not get my lunch earlier and am going to order something now. You are welcome to join me."

"Let me," I said, with respect, "place an order for the three of us." I did so at the bar and then returned to the vacant chair.

"I will not waste your time, Holmes," said Lestrade. "Nor will I waste mine. Let me get to the point immediately. I assume that you have read the latest in the press about the vanishing of these two youths and all the speculation that has accompanied it."

Holmes nodded, muttered his affirmation, and responded. "As with all accounts in the press, the facts are most likely highly distorted with the intent of selling more newspapers. Pray you, sir, give me the account as it is now known to Scotland Yard. Just the facts, please, sir, just the facts."

"Right." He paused, apparently ordering the facts inside his head before delivering them.

"Right, it goes this way. I will start with the family. The father is Mr. Samuel Cushing, a senior man in the Foreign Office. Highly respected. Cambridge. Been in the Service for over thirty years. His wife, Mrs. Sarah Cushing, is somewhat younger and comes from a family with money. They live on Ennismore Gardens, just a few blocks west of here. Just a normal, respectable, English commoner's family with only a couple of exceptions.

"The first is their religious persuasion. They are devout adherents of the sect we call the Darbyites and very strict in their moral behavior and their abstinence from all known pleasant human vices. Not even a pinch of honeydew tobacco can cross their threshold. The second is that Mr. Cushing has an identical twin. Not only that, but the other brother also had a distinguished career, however, in the Home Office. He passed away just over a year ago. Cushing, his wife, his brother and his wife, all four of them, had revolved their lives around the endless meetings at their local Gospel Hall up in Bayswater."

"Interesting," Observed Holmes. "And the help? Anything about their household staff?"

"We have learned," said Lestrade, "to always inquire about them, and so we did. There are some peculiarities, and these have given rise to yet more rumors and speculation in the press, and I must confess, among some of our police officers."

"Yes," said Holmes. "Please keep going, Inspector."

"It is not uncommon among wealthy families of some of the reformist religious sects to treat their employment of help as part of what they call their "ministry." Instead of working with reliable placement services and securing letters attesting to the character of maids and butlers and the like, they work through their church networks, or they contact some of our rescue missions who are busy helping drunkards, former criminals, and fallen women to recover and establish decent lives."

"Yes," I interjected. "There are some excellent charities doing good work there. Those dear ladies over at the Elizabeth Fry Society are truly angels in the prisons of the land."

"They may well be, Doctor," acknowledged Lestrade, "but the Cushings have chosen to associate only with those charities who share their peculiar religious convictions. The maid, a buxom, pretty lass, at one time worked on the streets of the East End as a prostitute but was brought, as the Christian brothers and sisters say, to 'a saving knowledge of her Lord and Savior' as a result of being handed a gospel tract. The cook is an invalid, minus an arm and an eye as a result of an accident in a factory. He was found in the poorhouse by one of their Christian philanthropists and taught to work in a kitchen, and from all reports, has become quite good at it. The man-servant, a former soldier, stumbled in drunk to a Sunday evening church service, came 'under the sound of the gospel'—whatever that is supposed to be, I do not know—and was saved and as a reward, I suppose, was given employment in the Cushing household. Again, all reports are in his favor.

"Beyond that, there is nothing to distinguish the Cushing family or their help from any other family on the block. The children, a boy and a girl, had reached sixteen and fifteen years respectively. Their names, biblically inspired, I believe, are Aaron and Miriam."

"Ah, yes," interjected Holmes. "Possibly the only brother and sister in the Scriptures after whom one would want to name your children. Either a Mary or a Martha could have been coupled with their brother Lazarus, but the Disciples lumped that poor chap in with fish and family who begin to stink after three days. And, for rather obvious reasons, Judah and Tamar would be unfortunate. So yes, Aaron and Miriam are a good choice for our devout family's children. Pray, continue, Inspector."

"Right. On Saturday, the lad and his sister attended a "youth fellowship" day at their church. Youth from the Gospel Halls throughout the London area get together for such functions once a fortnight in the summertime. As far as we can tell, they played a few games, had supper together, and ended the day with a Bible study and prayer session. At seven o'clock in the evening, they left the church and walked back home, as they did on all previous occasions, through Kensington Gardens and south to Knightsbridge.

"They never made it home. They would usually appear by eight. Their parents were not alarmed until ten o'clock had passed. At eleven, they went out to look for them, and at midnight they called for the police.

"Now, as I am sure you are aware, Holmes, the police get countless reports of young people who do not return home on Saturday evenings in the summertime. Invariably, they got into some harmless mischief, or they imbibed some forbidden beverage or fell asleep at a friend's home, or any such similar event, and we have learned not to become alarmed. They always manage to show up, shamefaced, at their parents' door before the end of the following day. The local constables considered this report just another one of the same, and regardless of the parents' protestations, did nothing other than sending one of their fellows on a walk-through Kensington in the middle of the night, which the officer found far more pleasant than sitting all night in the police station.

"Did he now?" asked Holmes pleasantly. "And what happened when the brother and sister failed to show up the following day?"

"The next morning, that being this Sunday past," said Lestrade, "the parents, as is their inviolable routine, attended the meetings at their church. They put the word out to all of the saints who were gathered there, asking them to report any knowledge they had. No one knew anything. So again they came to the police; this time directly to Scotland Yard. I will admit that at first, we were not particularly concerned. For a child in his or her teen years to be missing for two nights is worrisome to us, but again, more often than not, they have done only what we remember wanting to do when we were young, even if we never did. They have run off to Brighton and are romping on the beach, or they are at some sporting event, or some have even run off to Paris. If the girl had been by herself, we would have been more concerned, but she was with her older brother, and we reasoned that she most likely was safe. Adding to the lack of urgency was the fact, reported by the maid, that two suitcases were missing from the go-down, and many items of the children's clothing had been removed from their wardrobes."

"Which," said Holmes, "would support the contention of the police and the press that they had run off on a rebellious adventure."

"Correct," replied Lestrade. He said nothing for a few seconds and then added, "Then, in yesterday's post, these arrived."

He opened an envelope and handed Holmes two oversized playing cards. Holmes passed one of them on to me. I recognized them from my time in the service. They were tarot cards, and specifically the first and second cards of the Major Arcana, *The Magician* and *The High Priestess*. I knew that they were used commonly by fortune-tellers in their divinations but could not see any significance otherwise.

Holmes immediately pulled out his glass and spent several minutes with each of them. When he put them down, he turned to

Lestrade, and in a grave voice, asked, "Did anything else come in a later post? In a small box, perhaps?"

"Aha. You spotted it. Thought you might. Have to admit that I failed to until the box arrived, and then, sure enough, we saw it too."

"Please, both of you," I interjected. "What did you see?"

Holmes passed me his glass and the two cards. "Observe, carefully this time, the hands."

I did. Using the glass, I could see that on both the Magician and the High Priestess, the first fingers were missing. Someone had taken a fine scalpel and cut them out, leaving a small hole in the card. Suddenly a feeling of revulsion and horror swept over me.

"Oh my good Lord," I gasped. "What was in the box? Surely it was not what I fear."

"Yes, Doctor," said Lestrade. "It was exactly what you fear. Here it is. We are investigating a serious crime."

From his satchel, he procured a small yellow cardboard box and placed it on the table in front of us. He removed the lid, and inside I saw two human fingers. The fingers were not a pair. One was somewhat larger than the other and had a fingernail that was closely trimmed. The other, shorter and more slender, had a fingernail that was longer and carefully shaped. They were packed in salt. The end of them had been cleanly severed with a sharp instrument, most likely in one fell swoop.

"What sort of monster would do such a thing?" I said.

"To that," replied Lestrade, "I have no answer. However, you can now see why I sent for you."

"I do see," said Holmes. I looked at my friend. It was usual for his eyes to sparkle with anticipation when a new case was presented to him. That, however, was not the look I saw in his eyes this time. What I saw was alarm, fear perhaps. Urgency. The stern gravity of what was in front of us had hardened his features. I knew that every cell in his exceptional brain was on alert, every muscle in his body and every strand of emotion in his will had all been galvanized and were already fully engaged in the hunt.

In a slow, deliberate voice, he asked, "And was there any note, any demand received with these?"

"Not immediately with them," explained Lestrade. "In a later post, though, this note arrived."

He handed a second envelope to Holmes. I could see that it was addressed to Mr. Samuel Cushing, Ennismore Gardens, Knightsbridge. Holmes opened the envelope, removed the letter, and read it. He handed the envelope over to me as he did so. After several minutes, he retrieved the envelope from me and handed me the letter. Typed on the page were a few words:

```
One    thousand    pounds,    Mr.    Cushing,    or
everything  you  hold  near  and  dear  in  your
life will be destroyed.
```

Lestrade had learned, after many years of working with Sherlock Holmes, to be patient while Holmes looked over the evidence at hand. For five full minutes, nothing was said. Holmes then laid the letter and the envelope on the table.

"We have," said Holmes, "some leads to follow. Not terribly good ones, but a start."

"What leads? And just explain, Holmes," snapped Lestrade. "You know I have no time for any of your riddles."

"What little we have to begin with is this," Holmes said. "Tarot cards have been around for several hundred years, and there are countless versions and designs used by soothsayers, fortune tellers, and similar charlatans. But this specific design, with these pictures, is very new. It was released less than one month ago. The printing was done by the Rider Press. You can see their mark on the backside. The designs themselves were drawn by a professional illustrator, a Miss Pamela Smith. The project was sponsored by a fellow named Arthur Waite. The cards have never been used for any other reason. They are fresh and crisp. You can still smell the ink on them. They had not been removed from their box prior to being put to this awful use."

"Arthur Waite?" I queried. "Not that mystic fellow from up Islington way. He is quite the strange one, I hear."

"The same," said Holmes. "There was an announcement of the new printing three weeks back in one of our wretched tabloid newspapers. There are likely no more than a hundred of the decks sold to date, and most likely all to the community of clairvoyants. That is a broad field to sort through, but it is a start.

"The ransom demand was typed on a late-model Royal typewriter. There are thousands of them extant, but perhaps fewer that are also owned by occultists. The notepaper and envelope are of exceptional quality. Not the kind you would purchase at any general goods store, but one carried only by a select group of stationers. There are no more than a dozen such merchants in the city of London. It is not at all certain that the kidnapper is from London, but it is a reasonable premise on which to begin our searches. And the typist is a man, not a woman. That is evident by the forcefulness with which the keys have been struck. That is all the evidence we had so far, but we may take it that the sender of this letter is the man we want.

"However, if you will permit me, Inspector, it is possible that more evidence may be found in the Cushing home, which is only a few blocks from here. I assume that in calling us to Knightsbridge, you did so with the intention of having us visit the home and the family."

"Right, again, Holmes. That was obvious. So yes, let us be on our way over there. The worst of the heat is gone from the day, and it will not kill us to walk."

Chapter Three

A Family Terrorized

THE EMPRESS.

Ennismore Gardens is a lovely neighborhood that is centered on a small park and located part way between Knightsbridge Road and Brompton Road. The row of four-story white brick houses, neat and trim, with whitened steps and black doors, are not quite as posh as those inhabited by our bluebloods in Mayfair and Belgravia, but they are not to be sneezed at all the same. The families who enjoy the view of the gardens and mature trees are mostly from the upper-middle classes, with well-paid positions in His Majesty's civil services, or among the barristers and solicitors of the Inner Temple. It struck me that an enterprising kidnapper might have done far better for himself by abducting one of the scions of our nobility than the children of a civil servant, and it occurred to me, as I am sure it had already to Holmes, that perhaps money was not the only factor involved.

The Cushing family lived on the west side of the Gardens in a substantial house. A police wagon was parked in front of the door, and a dozen of our parasitical press were huddled on the sidewalk. Lestrade had his carriage let us off as close to the door as possible. Holmes pulled his hat down over his forehead, and we moved quickly from the curb to the front door, hoping not to be recognized by our vultures from Fleet Street.

It was to no avail. No sooner had we passed than I heard a voice shout out, "Crikey! Isn't that Sherlock Holmes?"

"Aye. 'Tis," came a reply. "There's somethin' to this if the Yard is callin' in Sherlock Holmes."

Immediately questions were shouted at Holmes, mostly containing the presupposition that the children of this excessively religious family might have turned towards the pleasures of the flesh. We ignored them and entered the home.

A tall, slender man-servant led us through the house to the back section, where it was decidedly cooler, and into the library. There we sat and waited for the master and mistress of the house to join us. In the hallway and in the library, I had observed a variety of items adorning the walls. Several were framed and glassed posters bearing verses from the Bible. Others were paintings, some original oils, and others copies of scenes from the biblical narratives, or from some artist's imagining of the devotional life. In one large painting, the Lord was breaking bread with two of his followers who had astonishment written all over their faces. In another, an oversized Jesus had his hand on the shoulder of a well-formed young man who was steering a ship through a treacherous storm. Curiously, on the wall opposite the desk, there was a familiar print of Christ, but on each side were prints that had no spiritual connotation. One was quite well-known—*General Gordon's Last Stand*—in which Charles "Chinese" Gordon, defending the British garrison in Khartoum, is portrayed standing defiantly at the top of the stairs while the forces of the Madhi ascend, deadly spears in hand. The second was, I was quite sure, a portrait of the American clergyman, Henry Ward

Beecher. His presence seemed odd, given that he was known to be far-removed in his religious beliefs from those practiced by the Darbyite Brethren. I would have gone over for a closer look, but at that moment, Mr. and Mrs. Cushing entered the room.

Samuel Cushing was a fit man in his early fifties. He was somewhat taller than me and a little shorter than Holmes. He had a full head of hair that was once black and now speckled with shades of gray. His handsome face looked tired, and his eyes looked out over bags of weariness. His wife was obviously at least fifteen years younger than her husband. Even without a trace of powder or lipstick, it was apparent that she was a physically beautiful woman, a tall, brunette, and with eyes of an unusual grey-blue shade. The flesh immediately surrounding her eyes was reddened, and one could tell that she had been in tears shortly before our arrival. Her face was wan and pale. Both of these good people were under considerable duress.

We stood and greeted them as Lestrade performed the introductions. When Mr. Cushing heard the name "Sherlock Holmes," he turned immediately and looked in amazement at my colleague.

"My goodness," he exclaimed. "Is there really a Sherlock Holmes? I had thought you were nothing but a work of fiction, made up out of whole cloth by some scribbler for *The Strand*. Forgive me if I seem surprised that such a fabulous figure should exist in flesh and blood."

Holmes was not amused but graciously responded, "I assure you, sir, that I do indeed exist and that the stories of my accomplishments, somewhat sensationalized by my friend here, Doctor Watson, are factually true, all of them."

"You must be joking," said Mr. Cushing, incredulously. "The only one I ever read, and I remember it clearly, told of some bizarre doctor who had a pet snake that he had trained to sip milk from a saucer, then go and bite someone and kill them, and then, upon hearing a whistle, return through the air vent to his little home inside a metal safe. Since no such creature has ever or could ever exist, the story was patent nonsense, of the same order as the American writer, Poe, and his monstrous shaving ape who decapitated the neighbors, but was then identified by some pedantic Frenchman named Lupin. Anyone who believes such lunacy belongs in Bed'lam."

I could see Holmes's entire body tensing. A touch of *sangfroid* deep within my soul made a point of remembering this incident for future reference. Given the gravity of the reason for our visit, I also refrained from mentioning to Mr. Cushing that his peculiar Christian sect firmly believed in the literal account of a talking snake that might not have been trained to sip milk but had successfully seduced a naked woman by way of an apple.

Sherlock Holmes smiled and, discretion being the better part of valor, moved on to the matters at hand.

"I know sir, and lady, that you are in a state of terrible stress and worry for your children and all I can do is promise you that I will devote my abilities, which I assure you are not fictional, to finding your children and returning them safely to you."

When he wanted to, Holmes could be quite authoritative and convincing. He spoke with such firm assurance that the parents relaxed and bid us be seated. For the next half hour, Lestrade and Holmes questioned them gently but thoroughly concerning their children and the events leading up to their now apparent abduction. I took copious notes.

When the interview had concluded, Holmes bowed ever so slightly toward the Cushings and spoke in a humble tone of voice.

"Forgive me for making such an ill-mannered request. It is a terrible invasion of your privacy, but I have found it very useful at times to conduct a thorough examination of the residence of the people involved in a crime. May I please, with your permission, inspect all corners of your home. You have my word that nothing I discover will be spoken of beyond the ears of the people gathered in this room."

Mrs. Cushing signed and responded. "By all means, sir. If you think it would be of any use, please proceed. We have nothing to hide from anyone. I cannot think of anything you will discover that would be of any help in rescuing our son and daughter, but go right ahead, and may God give you guidance."

"In that case, I may leave you here," said Lestrade, "for I have another small business at hand. I shall meet you back at Paxtons Head in an hour and a half. Does that give you sufficient time, Holmes?"

"It does indeed."

Lestrade departed, and Holmes went about his task, leaving me alone in the library. That was all well with me as I needed the time to add many more details to my notes about this gruesome case, but I had only a few minutes to myself before Mr. Cushing returned.

"Dr. Watson," he said with a forced smile, "I have totally forgotten my manners and abandoned a guest under my roof. Even under such trying circumstances, such a breach of etiquette should not be excused. We do not have any alcoholic spirits in this house but, please, let me offer you a cup of tea. Perhaps a sweet to go with it?"

I was about to refuse his offer and return to my welcomed moments of solitary work, but when I looked to respond with words to that effect, I found myself looking into the face of a man whose visage I had seen countless times before from so many men who had walked into my medical office. It was the face of a man whose soul was in turmoil, who needed no medical treatment, but who had a burning need to sit and talk to another man, bare the burdens of his heart, and simply be listened to *sans* judgment.

"A cup of tea would be splendid," I said. "But only if you will join me. I think a quiet cup might be just what the doctor ordered."

He smiled, unfeigned this time, and pulled on the bell cord.

"Let me have Browner organize a pot and something to go with it."

The same tall man-servant who had met us at the door appeared, stood at attention, and clicked his heels together.

"Yes, sir. You rang, sir."

"Ah, Browner, my good man. I am your employer, not your commanding officer. Your years in Her Majesty's Forces are showing yet again. Please, just a pot of tea and a plate of sweets for Doctor Watson and me, if you would be so kind."

"Right away, sir." He clicked his heels again and stopped his hand part-way to his forehead as if he was going to salute. He spun around and marched out of the room and down the hall.

Mr. Cushing was shaking his head slowly. "From a military family. He has only recently joined my staff. Spent some fifteen years in the B.E.F., and I fear they have got him to the very marrow of his bones. But enough of my eccentric household help, Doctor. Might I offer you anything to read while you are waiting? As you can see, these shelves are filled with excellent books."

I knew full-well that he did not want to give me a book and then depart, so I initiated a conversation with an observation that I thought might give him an opening to begin to chat, minus his inhibitions.

"I have, indeed, been admiring your books, sir, but I must confess it is the plaques, photographs, and paintings on your wall that I find intriguing."

"Ah, yes, those," he said, seeming to welcome the opportunity of respite from the terrible travail of the day by engaging in idle chitchat. "I have placed some items on my walls so that when I look up from my desk, I have forcible reminders of my human frailty and my constant need for dependence on the Word and the Lord."

The print of Jesus I could understand in that context, but Rev. Beecher and General Gordon baffled me.

"How in the world do an American preacher and a dead British General enhance your spiritual condition?" I asked, in innocent bewilderment.

He leaned back in his chair and looked up at the items to which I had referred.

"Since you are a doctor, sir, I suppose I can be frank and confess that the portrait of Rev. Beecher is there to remind me of the constant necessity to keep my physical appetites, or I should say, my sexual appetites, under close guard lest they destroy everything I have tried to build up over my lifetime. Beecher, you may recall, was an exceptionally gifted evangelist who was used powerfully by God not only to call sinners to salvation but to help right the dreadful wrong of slavery in America. He could have continued to have a wonderful ministry and perhaps even have become president of the United States had it not been for his giving in to the weaknesses of the flesh and having an affair with the wife of his friend and colleague. His example serves as a constant admonishment to all of us to be on the alert against such temptations and to be clad daily in the full armor of God so that we might be protected from the wiles of the evil one.

"The print of the death of General Gordon is a much more directly personal reminder, Doctor. Thirty years ago, when I was an ambitious up-and-coming officer in the Foreign Service, I was promoted beyond my years to hold the desk for Egypt and the Sudan. General Gordon was sent to Khartoum to evacuate the British garrison and leave the Sudanese natives to their fate at the hands of the Mahdi rebels. He bravely refused to follow those orders, and he stayed and protected the city and all its inhabitants. For a full year, he held out, and he kept sending requests for reinforcements, which were available up in Egypt and could have been sent to relieve his men and secure the city. His requests landed on my desk, and it was my job to forward recommendations directly to Prime Minister Gladstone, who kept the portfolio of Foreign Secretary for himself. I knew what the Prime Minister and his Cabinet wanted to hear. They detested General Gordon. He was an ardent Conservative and a favorite of Benjamin Disraeli. They were determined to make an example of him so as to assert their authority over Her Majesty's Forces. They wanted reasons to ignore his pleas, and I gave them what they wanted to hear. In my heart, as well as in my head, I knew the truth, and I chose to ignore it and seek the favor of men instead.

"You know what happened, Doctor Watson. Popular opinion eventually was so enraged by Gladstone's arrogance that he gave in and sent the requested relief. They arrived two days after the Mahdi rebels had stormed the city, murdered General Gordon, and savagely killed over ten thousand of the inhabitants who had been loyal to the British Empire. The carnage was brutal. Our soldiers and our loyal natives were tortured and had terrible things, too dreadful to speak of, done to them."

Here he paused, gazing again at the painting.

"Their blood is, at least to some extent, on my hands. I will have to answer at the last judgment for my actions, and I will have to, again, confess that I heeded my own selfish ambition instead of doing what I knew to be right, regardless of the personal consequences. Since that day, I have, with the Lord's help, tried to the best of my ability never to make that error again. I have steadfastly held out for doing what I believed to be the right thing, often against the concerted will of short-sighted politicians and greedy commercial interests. There has been a price to pay for it, but over time it has won me the respect of my peers and has given me a clear conscience with which to fall asleep every night. Having General Charles Chinese Gordon staring down at me every day is a constant and painful reminder I have given to myself that I must never, never again let down my guard and sacrifice my eternal integrity for the temporal praise of men."

I nodded my agreement and conveyed my genuine admiration of his record. We chatted some more about some of the other pictures on the walls, and then about his children. He was very proud of them. And then we turned to the matter at hand, and he just shook his head and admitted that he was entirely in the dark and simply could not understand what had happened.

Eventually, Sherlock Holmes returned from his inspection of the home and fetched me from the library. We bid our good evening to Mr. and Mrs. Cushing and walked the few blocks through Knightsbridge back to Paxtons Head.

Chapter Four

What Holmes Discovered

THE EMPEROR.

Lestrade was waiting for us.

"Speak up, Holmes," said Lestrade. "What of interest did you find? You always find something. Enlighten me."

Holmes slowly lit his pipe and took several puffs on it, and then a slow pull on his ale, followed by several more puffs. He and Lestrade had been at each other in their games of tit-for-tat for close on to two decades. There was no sign of a peace settlement on the horizon.

"They are a very fine lot," he began. "An unusual aspect of their beginning as a family was their wedding. Did you notice the photographs on the mantle in the library? Not only does Mr. Cushing have an identical twin, so does his wife. And the two identical twin brothers married the two identical twin sisters. We have to assume that the respective husbands and wives learned to identify one from the other or all manner of strange things might have occurred."

"We are not here," said Lestrade, "to speculate on prurient possibilities. What did you find that could shed light on the abduction of the children?"

"Ah, yes. I am coming to that. Your patience, please, Inspector. Mr. Cushing opened his file drawer to me in which he kept all of his records since he was a callow youth. He has assiduously accounted for every cent he has earned and spent for forty years. Although he did not refer me to it, I did note that he had tithed his gross income and then some, without fail. His tithe was donated to his Christian Assembly, and many additional gifts were given to various missions and charities that provide life's necessities for the indigent. He is a man of impeccable moral rectitude.

"His dear wife, as far as I could see, is of the same stock. She is blessed with an abundance of material wealth from her family but also gives alms to the poor and regularly participates as a volunteer not only with the church but with Bernardo's Homes, George Mueller's orphanages, The Royal Society for the Blind, and the Royal Humane Society. She has received, but does not display, numerous silver plates and other tokens of recognition for her service to humanity. These were all wrapped up and stored inside the bed storage box in her room. A very fine, modest lady indeed."

"Is this account going somewhere, Holmes," said Lestrade, cutting in. "What about the children? Any evidence of wild oats being sown?"

"Surprisingly, no. Their school records were entirely positive, praising them not only for their academic achievements but also for their character and their athletic abilities. The boy, Aaron, was the captain of the harrier team and had several ribbons to attest to his endurance and success. The girl, Miriam, was a member of the school track and field team and excelled at the hundred-yard dash. They had many citations from their church youth organizations and had spent all of the past month of July with the Scripture Union mission, handing out tracts and helping in vacation Bible schools.

"Right," said Lestrade. "Just what we would expect from young people who devote themselves to prayer and Bible study. But not a clue about their vanishing."

"My dear Inspector, I just gave you a very significant piece of evidence."

"You did nothing of the sort, Holmes. What evidence?"

"Inspector, did you not listen to me? I pointed out to you that both of them *could run.*"

Lestrade was silenced. He shook his head, took a sip of his ale, and responded. "Yes, Holmes, I suppose you did. And if they were accosted while walking back through Kensington Gardens, it must either have been by a group of men who suddenly overpowered them, or by someone they knew and trusted. At the very least, someone they did not run away from. The lawns in the Gardens are wide open. Unlikely anyone could have caught up with them. Very interesting, Holmes. Right. Anything else?"

Here Holmes moved his body in such a way as said to me that he was not entirely at ease with what he was about to say.

"This next observation is only speculation, and I hesitate to make it so early on and without anywhere near sufficient data."

"Right," said Lestrade. "Get on with it anyway. We are not here to pander to your moral scruples."

"Although it is beneath the dignity of a gentleman to do so, I examined in some detail the lady's toiletries, dressing closet, and even her lingerie."

"Blimey, Holmes," sneered Lestrade, "you are getting downright strange. So, what did you find?"

"The lady refrains from any use of lipstick, powders, or other cosmetics, and has only a few small, howbeit expensive, pieces of jewelry. But she does make use, to a very limited degree, of perfume."

"For Pete's sake, Holmes. Get on with it. I'm getting old waiting," said Lestrade.

"She uses *Mille Fleurs,* and only that brand and no other. It is one of the more popular of the high-end perfumes. Her clothing, her pillow, her bed linen all bore that faint but unmistakable scent."

"Holmes, I'm waiting."

"Her husband's clothes, but to a lesser degree, all had the same scent attached to them, which is to be expected. What was not expected was that some of his suits and shirts also had a very faint scent of Yardley's Lavender."

Here Holmes paused, waiting until the importance of what he had just said sunk in.

"Good heavens, Holmes," I gasped. "You cannot be suggesting that he has been so physically close to another woman as to acquire the scent of her bodily soaps and perfumes."

"I fear, my friend, that is exactly what I am suspecting."

"What about the daughter?" demanded Lestrade. "She's just fifteen, but that's when some young women today start to spread their wings and get a little bit of you-know-what in their blood."

"I examined the daughter's boudoir as well. And yes, the young lady has started to use some perfume. Secreted away in her closet was a small bottle that was only half full."

"Was it Lavender?" I asked. "A loving father would be expected to give his daughter a tender embrace from time to time."

"As he should, of course," replied Holmes. "But alas, no, it was *Jockey Club,* the brand most prized by young women today who are intent on asserting their femininity."

All three of us sat in silence for the next several minutes, not at all sure about what to do with the information we had acquired.

"I suggest, my friends," said Holmes, "that we install this data in the backs of our minds until we know more. However, it does open to us the possibility of actions driven by passions, jealousy, and revenge. These all too often overtake reason and even greed as motives for the most diabolical of crimes."

Lestrade and I nodded our agreement and, the discussion having concluded, we returned to our abodes for the evening.

I spent the next day at my medical practice, attending to my patients. At the end of the day, since my dear wife had not returned from depleting my bank account up north of the River Ribble, I hastened back to 221B Baker Street. It was still a hot August day, but the heat had gone out of the afternoon by the time I climbed the familiar seventeen steps and was greeted by the indefatigable Mrs. Hudson. She sat me down and returned a minute later with an iced lemonade. I remarked yet again to myself how lucky Sherlock Holmes had been to find such a woman who, having determined that Holmes was the most dreadful tenant in all of London, still not only put up with him but positively doted on the chap.

"Mr. Holmes," she said, "went out early this morning and has not returned. He did say that he would be back by suppertime, so I have it prepared and waiting. I expect him shortly."

She hardly had these words out of her mouth when I heard the door on Baker Street open and then the thuds of Holmes bounding up the stairs two at a time.

"Merciful heavens," I said as he entered the room. "You must have had a rewarding day. Have you found the missing children?"

"Oh, no. Not yet. But I have had excellent results from my hours of plodding and slogging. Tomorrow we have a very good chance of identifying the kidnapper. Or, possibly the day after tomorrow. But he is within my grasp. It will not be long."

Over a plate of Mrs. Hudson's perfectly poached salmon, he chatted on happily about his various escapades. He had started with the stationery, the very refined writing paper on which the ransom demand was written.

"It took several hours, but I was able to assemble a list of all of the shops that sell that quality of paper. It is a linen base, not mere pulped wood, and costs at least two pence a page. There are, in fact, only ten shops in all of London that sell it. Of course, it might have been purchased in another city, but I think that unlikely. I was able to visit several of the shops before they closed for the day and eliminate five. That leaves me only five to return to tomorrow and secure from them their list of recent customers for this very peculiar purchase. Then we shall move on and find the fellow."

In between forkfuls of salmon, and swallows from a bottle of claret, he would occasionally rub his hands in unfettered glee. When dinner ended, we retired to our chairs in front of the unlit hearth, and he poured a generous brandy for both him and me.

"To your health, Doctor. And to the relentless pursuit of justice."

Holmes then spent the next few minutes talking about nothing other than violins, narrating with great exultation how he purchased his own Stradivarius. This led him to Paganini and anecdote after anecdote about that extraordinary man who played with such inhuman skill that his listeners, in wonderment, thought him possessed by the devil.

His good humor did not last long.

A knock came to the door on the street, and we listened as someone plodded slowly up the stairs. Lestrade entered the room. His shoulders were slouched over, and his countenance was grim.

Without a word, he withdrew an envelope from his suit pocket, opened it, and placed two more tarot cards on the table. From my chair, I could see that they were the next two cards of the Major Arcana, *The Emperor* and *The Empress*. I reached for one and Holmes for the other.

"Oh, no. Oh, no," I muttered, choking on my words as a sickening feeling swept over me. The left hand of both figures had been cut out, leaving small holes in the cards. Lestrade then opened his valise, took out a cardboard box, and placed it on the table beside the cards. It was about a foot square and four inches in depth.

"Open it," he said, his voice flat and emotionless. I did so, fearing the worst and, a second later, having those fears confirmed. Inside the box were two human left hands. They were packed in salt, but even without brushing it away and making a close examination, I could see that one was from a young woman, the other a young man.

Holmes sat back in his chair, his lower lip was trembling slightly. He made no effort to take out his glass or look at the horrific items in front of us.

"Was there," he said in a whisper, "any demand note? Anything?"

"No. Nothing."

"Any other markings on the box beyond what is here now?"

"No. None."

"Thank you, Inspector. I appreciate your bringing the evidence over to me. If you will permit me to examine it, it can then be taken to the morgue."

"That's why I brought it."

"Yes, of course. Thank you."

"Inspector," I said, "What of the family? They must be in dire straits."

"They are, and it is most understandable. They cannot leave their door without being besieged by the press. Somehow it became known that the maid was what the press call a 'Gladstone Girl'—you recall that our Prime Minister used to prowl the streets of Whitechapel searching for young prostitutes that he could rescue—and questions are being shouted to these devout people about their operating a brothel and all that sort. It has not helped that the maid failed to come to work this morning and has possibly returned to her former profession. I have stationed two constables at the doorway to make sure that friends may enter and leave without being impeded. Unfortunately, I can do nothing about the provocative shouts and murmurs.

"I am not, as you know, Holmes, in the habit of darkening the door of any church, established, Romish, or otherwise, but I do give due credit to the friends of the family. They have been visiting them constantly, bringing food and offering to help in whatever is needed. And, of course, having constant prayer meetings. But even with that, the pain and suffering of the parents is pitiable."

"I can well imagine," said Holmes. He then went on to explain what progress he had made in tracking down the source of the notepaper used by the kidnapper for the ransom letter. The police inspector and the consulting detective then parted for the evening, promising to keep each other informed of any advances.

The following morning, I rose at an early hour, only to find that Holmes had already had a coffee and departed the house. I was not surprised. It was in his character that once he set upon the scent of a criminal, he stopped at nothing in his dogged pursuit. I had known him to go for several days with no sleep, little food, and sustained for the most part by coffee and tobacco.

I spent the day in my medical practice, returning in the early evening to a solitary supper that Mrs. Hudson had dutifully prepared.

"I'll leave some cold cuts out for Mr. Holmes," she said. "Goodness only knows when he'll get in. If you are still up when he does, Doctor, do try to get him to eat something."

I promised that I would and waited up until near eleven o'clock before I heard Holmes familiar tread on our stairs. I greeted him, insisted that he be seated, and placed the food in front of him. To my relief, he ate at least a portion of it before pushing the plate back away.

"So," I began, quite casually. "What news? Have you found the kidnapper's stationer?"

He lit a cigarette, inhaled, and sighed. "I do believe I have. It was nothing brilliant on my part; merely the eliminating of all the other possible shops until only one remained. I visited there at the end of the day and confirmed that they did indeed carry this line and color of writing paper and envelopes and that they had sold a package of it recently. Unfortunately, it was only a shop-girl on duty, and she did not have access to the records. The proprietress was gone for the day, but I am told that she comes in early in the morning. Tomorrow morning, I will be there to greet her when she does."

"Well done, my friend," I said, trying to offer some encouragement to my weary companion. "Anything else?"

"Yes. The family received another ransom note. Lestrade has it, but he showed it to me. The perpetrator of this horrible crime has upped his demand to two thousand pounds and has given a bank account in Zurich into which the funds must be paid within two days, or, to quote from the letter 'All hell will descend upon you and your family.'"

"But were there any other …" I hesitated to say more.

"More cards, or body parts?" Holmes anticipated my question. "No, for which I assume we should be thankful."

He said no more, retired to his chair, and lit up another cigarette. I sat in silence across from him, rising only to retrieve the plate of food from the table and place it on the coffee table in front of him.

At eleven-thirty, we rose to retreat to our bedrooms when there was a loud banging on our door. We both looked at each other in bewilderment, and I hastened down the stairs and opened it.

I could see no one, but on the doorstep was a box, elegantly tied with a wide red ribbon, and with an envelope attached under it. I picked it up, brought it up the stairs and into our parlor, and placed it on our coffee table, beside the still uneaten plate of food.

Holmes looked at it blankly for a short time and then leaned forward and took the envelope. I watched as he opened it. The look of pain that invaded his face was message enough. He withdrew two more tarot cards and placed them on the table. They were the next two in the Major Arcana suit, *The Hierophant* and *The Lovers*. My hand trembled as I picked them up. The right foot of the Hierophant had been cut out, as had the right foot of the female lover.

I sat motionless for a minute, then took a deep breath and reached for the box. I looked up at Holmes, and he nodded. I slowly undid the ribbon and removed the lid. Inside, covered in salt, were two severed right feet. One obviously belonging to a young man, the other to a young woman. There was a note placed beside them.

"Read it, please, Doctor," said Holmes, his voice drained of all emotion.

It ran:

```
Dear Sherlock Holmes: Wasn't it good of me
to spare your fellow incompetent,
Lestrade, the trouble of bringing these to
```

you. Please enjoy the pain. It is your
payment for interfering.

"Might I prevail upon you, my dear friend," he said to me, "to come with me first thing tomorrow morning? And perhaps you could bring your service revolver with you."

Chapter Five

Following the Paper Trail

THE HIEROPHANT

he sun rose the following morning shortly after six o'clock. Half an hour later, we were out of 221B Baker St., having given breakfast a pass, and in a cab on our way to the elegant, exclusive shops of the West End. Neither Holmes nor I frequented this area often, the prices being well beyond the means of our pocketbooks. The object of our investigation, however, appeared to have rich tastes, and our presence on Bond Street was required.

At seven o'clock, the cab discharged us at the corner of Bond and Burlington Gardens. The sign above the shop we were approaching read *Missolonghi's – Stationery and Fancy Goods Emporium.*

"This is the only shop," Holmes explained again, in case I have forgotten our conversation from the night before, "that sells the particular brand of notepaper, and that has, in the past two weeks, sold a packet in the particular color used by our monster. I am hoping that the good lady who owns the establishment has kept a record of her customers, as should all select shops that cater to an elite clientele."

The shop had not yet opened for business, but by peering through the window, we could see an elegantly dressed woman setting out the displays of her wares on the counters. Holmes tapped on the glass, got her attention, and beckoned her to open the door.

"Well, my goodness," she exclaimed, "aren't you two chaps eager this morning. Let me guess; today is the wedding anniversary of one of you, and you forgot until you woke up this morning, and now you are in a panic lest your wife be devastated yet again by your hopelessly unromantic behavior."

She laughed merrily as she spoke and gestured to us to enter. "Well, come on in, gentlemen. You are not the first, nor will you be the last that I have had to save from well-deserved punishment. I would guess that neither of you has even had breakfast yet. There is some coffee and some sweet breads in the back office. Have a seat, and I will bring some, and you can tell me your desperate tale of woe."

She gestured to us to be seated on an elegant sofa and glided her way toward the back of the store.

"I fear," I said *sotto voce,* "that we will disappoint her when all we ask for is information about her customers."

"Not at all," said Holmes, with the first trace of a smile I had seen on his face for days. "If I remember correctly, this coming Saturday is your wedding anniversary, and you have totally forgotten about it, haven't you? Your dear Mary will be returning from Blackpool, and you had better have something elegant to express your undying love and how awfully you have missed her."

I was speechless. "Oh my goodness," I whispered, "you are right. Thank you. But the goods in this emporium are far beyond my means. Just a simple set of earrings would set me back a hundred pounds."

"Well then, you had better ask about their elegant packages of writing paper."

The lady who had greeted us returned bearing a platter with a flask of coffee and some delectable rolls and pastries and set them in front of us.

"And might you," Holmes inquired graciously, "be Mrs. Missolonghi, the owner of this fine establishment?"

She laughed again. "Oh, no, no. I am the owner, but my name is Tiffany Barnes. However, if you are not in too great a rush this morning, I will tell you how the store was named. It is a most amusing story, or, at least, it is to some people."

"I am all attention," said Holmes. I knew from years of observing him that he invariably extracted more information from people from all walks of life by friendly conversation and genuine interest in them than would ever have happened had he been belligerent and demanding.

"I must admit," he continued, "I find it quite a puzzle to understand how a lovely lady named in honor of a posh shop in New York City, came to be the owner of a posh shop in the West End, named after some obscure village in Greece, made famous for being the last place on earth where Lord Byron was, if I may say, being Byronic."

"Oh, how splendid," she exclaimed, clapping her hands together. "A learned man. Well then, sir, whoever you are, it so happens that both my mother and father were, in their youth, hopeless Romantics and entirely besotted with the poetry and stories of Lord Byron. Yes, the one who was 'mad, bad, and dangerous to know.' They came from excellent families but were a bit wild at heart and took themselves on grand tours of the Continent, and made a pilgrimage to Missolonghi, in the south of Greece, to pay homage at the place where their hero died his tragic death. They met each other there and within an hour had fallen in love. They found a Greek priest to marry them in some old chapel on the shores of the Aegean Sea. On their wedding night, my father read Byron's poetry to my mother, which, I have to assume, positively threw her into heat, and nine months later, I arrived on this planet, beginning my life on some pleasant island in the Mediterranean. I was born on the feast of Epiphany, and in keeping with Greek custom, I was named Theophania. Since that was just too much Greek for their families, they settled on the English version, 'Tiffany.' And so here I am, and quite pleased to have two fine gentlemen in my store so early on a summer morning. But permit me, kind sirs, who is it that I have the pleasure of assisting at this early hour?"

"My name is Sherlock Holmes. This is my colleague, Dr. John Watson."

The woman again clapped her hand in front of her bosom. Then repeated the gesture, causing her sparkling diamond necklace to bounce up and down. "Oh my! Oh my! *The* Sherlock Holmes has come to my shop. Oh my! How wonderful. Does this mean that my store is going to be in one of your stories, Dr. Watson? Is somebody about to be murdered here? Oh my! Think of the traffic that would create. That would bring record sales. Oh my! How utterly gorgeous. Or did some foolish husband buy some lovely diamonds for his mistress? And his wife found out? Did she poison him? Oh my! Do tell. What happened? This is beyond my dreams. The shop will be overrun with the curious. All those bluebloods just cannot resist a mystery, especially if diamonds are involved. It would all be so … well … so deliciously *Byronic*. My mom and dad would be so proud of me. Oh please, do tell, sir. What has brought Sherlock Holmes into my shop?"

I was at a loss for words, and briefly, so was Sherlock Holmes. He recovered, cleared his throat, and replied in his practiced gracious manner.

"My dear Miss Tiffany, you are correct in deducing that my visit is part of an investigation, and we are in need of your help. Please understand that the matter is extremely delicate and I am precluded from giving any details. I can, however, promise, that should you be able to help us, my colleague, Dr. Watson, will most certainly give full credit to you and your shop."

She beamed back at him and, yet again, clapped her hands. "Well then, sir, just ask away. I never imagined that someday I might be interviewed by Sherlock Holmes. Oh, it is such a shame that our photographer is not here. Having a photo of you looking in through the shop window while sipping your coffee would be such a splendid advert in the *Times*. But that cannot be helped. Just go ahead with your questions, Mr. Holmes."

Holmes leaned forward and looked directly as Miss Tiffany Barnes. I took out my notebook, ready to take down every word.

He pulled out the note that bore the ransom demand and handed it, with the writing side down, to the lady.

"I believe that you sold a packet of this fine stationery during the past fortnight, did you not?"

"Yes, I did. I remember it exactly. It was on the Monday of the week before last. Well, possibly it was the Tuesday. Not really sure what day. But I do remember the fellow who bought it. Fine looking gentleman. Nicely dressed. His suit was most certainly an Italian cloth, sold only on Saville Row. His handkerchief was Chinese silk. It differs from the Indian variety and has a finer weave. White, it was. Yes. Or was it ivory? Oh pooh, the color is not important. What mattered is that it was top drawer Chinese, and not something from the Punjab. He asked for a simple package of stationery. Well, I took one look at him, and I knew right away that I was not going to sell him just any old bunch of paper and envelopes. No, sir. I could see that he had very fine taste and so I brought out our most expensive line. Fine linen. Twenty-four pound it was. He paid for it with a five-pound note and waved me away when I offered him the change. And then he departed. Yes, sir. I remember him exactly."

"Did he give you his name?"

"Oh no sir, we never ask for names when gentlemen come in her unaccompanied by their wives. Why all sorts of chaps come here to buy gifts for their mistresses, and they do so having full trust in our ability to protect their anonymity. So no sir, of course, we did not ask for his name."

I could see Holmes countenance and body become more tense, but he put on his friendly face and continued.

"Miss Tiffany, it is of critical importance that we locate this man. It is a matter of life and death. Please try to remember anything else you can about him."

"Honestly, Mr. Holmes, I have told you everything I can remember about the fellow." She stopped and looked distressed. I perceived that she might have imagined her role in a mystery story vanishing.

"I am so sorry, sir, that I have no idea who he was. But would it help if I gave you the address to which I had the package delivered?"

Holmes looked intently at her, and then his face relaxed into an unfeigned smile.

"Yes, miss, that would be most helpful."

"Oh, well, you should have said so, sir. We keep all the delivery addresses on record, just not the names of the men who make such purchases. Let me look it up for you."

She rose and retreated to the back office. She was gone for over five minutes, and when she reappeared, she was bearing yet another tray with coffee and pastries.

"Here you go, gentlemen. You enjoy another round while I look up the record."

From under the plate of pastries, she extracted a ledger book and opened it. She ran her finger down the page, muttering comments about the items and the purchasers as she did so. I poured us two more cups of coffee and enjoyed another portion of my breakfast.

"Oh, oh! Here it is. Yes. Here. Look. On Thursday of two weeks ago: one package of Vergé of Paris. They have a very select line, they do. Delivered to 85 Montpelier Square, Knightsbridge. Oh now, wasn't that ducky? He came all the way to us instead of just dropping into Harrods's. A man with very demanding taste. Do you not agree, Mr. Holmes? Is that of some help to you, sir?"

"It is indeed, Miss. Very helpful. You may have helped solve a terrible crime and even prevent a murder."

One more time, she clapped her hands and beamed with joy.

Having finished our breakfast at Tiffany's we walked toward to door. As we did, Holmes whispered to me.

"There is a man standing on the pavement who has been observing us while we have been in here. As soon as we exit, turn right and try to catch him. And, by the way, you forgot to buy your anniversary gift."

The fellow he was referring to must have sensed that Holmes had noticed him, for as we opened the door, he sprang across the street and into the driver's seat of a parked carriage. He laid a whip upon the haunches of the horse, and it bounded away, straight through the section of road repairs on Bond Street. The small carriage bounced and rattled as it raced across the potholes and piles of gravel. The driver had, although obviously shaken, not stirred from his perch and continued his escape. In the distance, I could see him turn right on Piccadilly and disappear in the direction of Green Park.

"Someone is on to us," said Holmes. "We have to move quickly."

We hailed a cab, and Holmes offered the driver a sovereign if he would race through the road construction and get us to Knightsbridge in less than ten minutes. The cabbie cooperated, and soon we were galloping along Piccadilly and passing Hyde Park Corner.

"What's the address?" shouted the cabbie.

I was about to shout back the number on Montpelier Square when Holmes put his hand on my arm and shouted out the address of the Cushing House on Ennismore Gardens.

"If the children are being held there, they will most likely be too terrified to reveal themselves to us, given what they have already endured. We will stop and pick up their father. They will know his voice."

We galloped further along Knightsbridge Road and around the corner onto Ennismore. Upon reaching the Cushing home, I leapt from the cab, happy to see that it was too early in the morning for the press to have gathered and pounded on the door. The butler opened it, and I barged past him into the parlor. There I stopped in my tracks. Seated in the room were Mr. and Mrs. Cushing, and Inspector Lestrade. Two constables were standing in the hallway. On the coffee table was a box, identical in size to the one delivered to Holmes the previous night. The ribbon was undone and lying loosely on the table. The top of the box was in place. I knew immediately what I was looking at.

I gathered my wits and spoke as forcefully as I could. "Please, Mr. Cushing and Inspector, come with me. Holmes is outside in a cab. We may have located the children. Please come now."

Lestrade and Mr. Cushing both jumped to their feet and raced out the door. I followed, stepped up into the cab as it pulled away from the curb. I dropped into the seat beside Lestrade, who leaned his head to my ear. "Cards seven and eight. *The Chariot* and *Strength*. The right hand and forearm."

We pulled to a sharp halt upon reaching the house on Montpelier. It was similar in many respects to the Cushing home a few blocks away, another fine four-story row house in Knightsbridge, facing onto a leafy square. Lestrade bolted from the cab and knocked firmly on the door. It was opened by a tall, grave-looking maid, with a very shiny cap, who expressed shock on hearing the inspector announce that he was from Scotland Yard.

"Where is your master?' demanded Lestrade.

"Sir," the distraught woman sputtered, "he is where he is every morning by this time. He is at his office, or maybe in court over in Temple Bar."

"And your lady?"

"She...she...sir, she is at the hairdresser. She has a luncheon today in Mayfair. I can send for here, sir. Do you wish me to do that?"

Lestrade stopped shouting. "No. No. That will not be necessary. Who is it we are looking for, Holmes?"

"Very sorry to intrude upon you, miss," said Holmes. "We are searching for a gentleman, about my height, most likely well-dressed, and we have reason to believe that he lives here."

"Oh," the poor woman sighed as her face and body relaxed. "You must mean Mr. Gulliver, the tenant. He rents the fourth floor from my master. But he is seldom here. He says he has plans in the future to set up a studio up there, but right now, there are only a few sticks of furniture and a small kitchen. I can show you up there, but he has not been around for several days."

The four of us pushed the poor soul aside and bounded up the stairs. The fourth floor was not much more than an attic, accessed by a steep, narrow stairway at the back of the house. The door was locked. Holmes reached into his pocket for the small set of locksmith tools he always carried with him. Lestrade shoved him aside, raised his leg and gave a powerful kick to the door, smashing the lock.

"There are some things the police are allowed to do that amateur detectives cannot," he said as he entered the rooms. We followed him, and within less than fifteen seconds, we had opened every door, every closet, and every cupboard. There was no one there.

We met in the front room, every one of us empty-handed. "Clearly, the children are not here," said Holmes. "However, the notepaper on the desk and the Royal typewriter tell us that we are in the right place. So, I suggest that all of us look for whatever evidence we can find that might be helpful in leading us to them."

Chapter Six

The Sins of the Father

THE LOVERS.

We nodded and began to look slowly through the cabinets, desk drawers, and wardrobes. I watched as Mr. Cushing opened the door of a wardrobe in the bedroom. Inside were several shirts and a couple of men's suits. On the floor were a pair of boots and two pairs of shoes. Mr. Cushing suddenly stepped back, and I saw a look of shock on his face. He turned and stepped quickly into the front room and walked to the desk that sat along the front wall beside the window. On top of the desk was a powerful set of field glasses. He picked them up and looked out. Then he slowly opened the central drawer of the desk and removed a large bulky envelope. From it, he extracted a handful of photographs. I could see the color draining from his face as he did so. He put them down and walked backwards slowly until he reached a chair. He sat down, placed his elbows on his knees and his head in his hands, and began to weep uncontrollably. His entire body was shaking, and his crying was pathetically loud for a grown man.

The wretched noises he was making immediately brought Holmes and Lestrade back into the room. I held up my hand and silently gestured to them to sit in the chairs that were on the other side of the room. They did so, and I picked up the stack of photographs that Mr. Cushing has so recently placed back on the desk. I looked at them one after the other before handing them on the Holmes and Lestrade.

They made no sense at all. All of them were of Mr. Cushing and his wife. The first ones in the pile were taken at the front door of his home on several occasions spanning the past winter and spring. In each, he was giving his wife an affectionate kiss. I assumed at first that he was leaving for work until I noticed that in the winter scenes, the streetlights had already been lit.

The others, farther down in the pile were very unseemly. They had been taken through the window of the house and were clearly photos of Mr. and Mrs. Cushing engaging in private acts such as are the pleasure of a loving married couple. The photos on the bottom of the pile left nothing to the imagination. It was all exceedingly perplexing.

I had noticed that in one of the kitchen cupboards, there was a bottle of a select brandy. I poured a generous glass and brought it to the poor man, who was still convulsing in grief.

"Sam," I said. "I do not care if this is forbidden by your church. Swallow it, take a few deep breaths, and then compose yourself."

He looked up. His face was contorted, and tears were streaming from his eyes. Without saying anything, he took the glass and swallowed the contents. I saw him take several deliberate deep, slow breaths. He raised his head and spoke, but very slowly.

"The man you are looking for is Alec Fairbairn."

"Go on, please, Sam," I said.

"He is my brother-in-law."

Holmes looked puzzled and spoke. "Your brother-in-law, I had understood, was also your brother. And he died last year. What are you saying?"

"No, my wife had two sisters. One, Mary, is her twin and was married to my twin brother, Seth. The four of us have been very close to each other for the past twenty years. There is a third sister, Susan. She is younger and is married to a chap named Alec Fairbairn."

"I am afraid," said Lestrade sharply, "that I do not see where this is going. Please enlighten me, sir. And do so quickly. Your children are still at risk and in mortal danger."

"Perhaps," interjected Holmes, "I can help you get started. The front door in the photographs is not your home, nor is the bedroom window. The woman with whom you are being intimate is not your wife, Sarah. It is your sister-in-law, Mary, the widow of your brother, Seth."

Cushing said nothing. He dropped his head back into his hands and nodded it slowly.

"And might it also be true," continued Holmes, "that there has been an estrangement between the four twins and the other sister and brother-in-law? Animosity, even?"

Cushing nodded again.

"Your brother-in-law somehow became aware of your affair and has blackmailed you, threatening to expose everything and ruin your well-respected life. And if I were to pick up the field glasses and look across the square, would I be looking directly at the front door of your deceased brother's home where his widow continues to live, and then into the window of her bedroom?"

Samuel Cushing raised himself up and looked directly at Holmes. "Yes sir, that is precisely what happened and what you would see."

None of us spoke, and then Lestrade nearly shouted at us.

"Good lord, that is no more than an everyday case of blackmail against some bloke who cannot keep his trousers on. We see that every day. How in the world do dismembered children fit into this? Where are they? Who is this monster of a brother-in-law that is not happy with a few thousand pounds? This makes no sense!"

"Sir," said Cushing quietly, turning to Lestrade. "For that, I have no answer. Alec and Susan grew up in the same Christian Assembly as Mary, Seth, Sarah and I did. They were in our wedding party and were married three years later. Yet immediately after they were removed from the authority of their parents' homes, they began to partake of the pleasures of the world. They were reported to have gone dancing together, to have attended raucous and obscene performances in the music halls. They passed their time with a whole group of ungodly friends in the local pub, and a little drink would send them into stark, raving, depraved utterances. They dabbled in devilish, occult practices. They even strayed so far from the straight and narrow as to place bets on horses at the racetrack. This became known to the elders of the Assembly, and they were visited and spoken to. There was no improvement, and the admonishment was repeated. They refused to change and even exulted in what they called their freedom. Sadly, it was necessary to read them out of fellowship."

"You mean you and all the good saints in your church shunned them?" said Holmes.

"Such an extreme action is only ever taken for the purpose of redemption and restoration," said Cushing. "However, they would have none of it. Perhaps they might have seen the error of their ways, but my father-in-law, Sarah and Mary's father, died, and when his will was read, we learned that he had cut them out entirely. Nothing was to be given to them. Not even the childhood dolls with which Susan had played. The four of us thought it terribly harsh and unfair, but

49

there was nothing that could be done about it. The terms of the will were explicit and binding. That ended any contact we had with them. Susan's temper was unleashed. To this day, we have not spoken."

"You still," snapped Lestrade, "have not explained how this Alec fellow could be such a monster."

Cushing looked stunned. "Sir, I have no answer for that. Alec was my friend growing up. He was outgoing, playful, perhaps attracted a bit much to the things of this world, but never, never one to injure another person. And that he would torture and maim my children, his niece and nephew, is beyond belief. Somehow…somehow, the evil one has taken his soul. I have no other explanation."

"This Alec chap," said Lestrade, "where do we find him?

Cushing gave us an address in Chelsea and then added, "He works for Barings in the City. But he does not usually depart from his home until near to ten each morning. You might meet him as he stepped out of his front door in a half-hour from now."

"My dear, Doctor," said Holmes, looking at me. "Might I prevail upon you to stay with Mr. Cushing and see him home? I believe he could use your support. The inspector and I will go looking for this monster."

I agreed. Holmes and Lestrade descended the stairs, and I sat with a man who just a fortnight earlier had been on top of his world. Now I was looking at a man who, I was quite sure, wanted nothing more than to die.

For several minutes, neither of us spoke, then I inquired, as gently as I could. "Sam," I said, "how could you, of all people, do anything so foolish as to have an affair with your sister-in-law? You had Rev. Beecher looking down at you every day, reminding you not to give in to the sins of the flesh. What happened?"

He looked vacantly out the window and then spoke to the sky beyond. "It is impossible to explain to anyone who has not been raised with an identical twin, how that can so alter every aspect of your life. As boys growing up, Seth and I wore the same clothes, played with the same toys, attended school and Sunday school together, played all the same games at the same time. People spoke to us as if we were the same person. We were treated as if we had only one identity, not two. By the time we were in our teens, we were thinking the same thoughts, finishing each other's sentences, and experiencing the same emotions, whether anger, or joy, or sorrow, or whatever. It was not as if we had only one identity. We knew we were distinct from each other. But we were certainly not complete without each other. Marrying twin sisters, who had grown up in almost the same context as we had was absolutely logical. All of us understood each other in that way, a way that no one who has not had a twin ever can.

"Seth died suddenly last year. The only way in which we were not identical was that he had a weak heart, and I did not. His heart failed last September, and he collapsed at his desk and was dead. It was a terrible shock to all of us. I was simply no longer a complete man. I prayed about it over and over again, but the void did not go away. My dear wife, Sarah, felt the pain and anguish of her sister in a way that again cannot be explained to someone who has not seen a twin endure pain and felt it along with her.

"I spent many hours in Seth's home, sorting out his estate and making sure that all his affairs were in order so that Mary could live comfortably. Seeing her in such pain was as if I was seeing my wife in that pain. I did what I would have done with Sarah and embraced her and let her cry against me. Soon we became intimate. Her face and body are exactly the same as my wife's. Mine are the same as her husband's.

"Somehow, it did not seem wrong, merely an extension of our marriages. I know that cannot make sense, but that is what happened.

It continued through the winter and into the spring. It has faded over the past few weeks as she has had to overcome her situation and face a new life without Seth. I know it was wrong. It was a sin before heaven and before my wife. Yet somehow, I feel no guilt. It was as if it were my duty."

"And how," I asked, "are you going to explain it to your wife?"

He said nothing. I watched his face contort, and again he buried his face in his hands. When he rose, he looked at me with an imploring look.

"Doctor Watson, I have only just met you, and I know that you are not my brother in the Lord nor even a close friend. But you now know more of me than any other man on earth. I know it is the coward's way out, but could I implore you, please, on my behalf, to go to my home and inform Sarah of all that has transpired. Please tell her everything. I will take a long walk through the Gardens and try to screw my courage to the sticking place and come home to her within two hours. Will you that for me, sir?"

There are some responsibilities that go with being a doctor, and this, though unexpected, was clearly one of them. I agreed, gave him a warm pat on the shoulder, and turned to depart. Before doing so, I reached over and handed him the bottle of brandy. "You would not be the first man to need a little liquid support," I said. "Nor will you be the last. You're a good man, Sam Cushing. You have a wife and children who now need you more than ever."

He took my hand and gave it a hard squeeze.

I walked slowly back to Ennismore Gardens, rehearsing what I was going to say with each slow step. I had learned in my many years in medical practice that the best way, indeed the only way, to impart devastating news to a patient was to speak the truth, the whole unvarnished truth, calmly, completely, and slowly, and then try to help in whatever manner was required by the reaction of my patient. I would do the same now.

I entered the home and was greeted again by the man-servant, Mr. Browner, and shown to the parlor. He inquired if I would like a cup of tea and perhaps some nourishment, and I gladly accepted. My breakfast at Tiffany's having now been several hours ago, I was hungry. Some ten minutes passed before Mrs. Sarah Cushing appeared and sat down across from me.

In a matter-of-fact way, I explained the events of the morning. I told her first the disappointing news concerning our failure to find the children, the shock of learning that the terrible culprit was her brother-in-law, Alec Fairbairn, and the truth of the content of the blackmail and of her husband's infidelity. As I concluded, I detected a look from her that I had not expected. There was a touch of anger in her eyes, and it was directed at me.

"Let us," she began in a firm voice, 'deal with the less significant matters first. You may think less of me for what I am about to tell you, Doctor Watson, and quite frankly, I do not care. However, I know and have known all along that my husband was giving intimate comfort to my sister. I wanted him to. I encouraged it. I made it as convenient as possible for him to do so."

I was stunned, and my face must have betrayed my reaction.

"Oh, please, doctor, do not look so nonplussed. Surely, you must know from the medical literature concerning identical twins that we are simply not the same as other people, not even as other brothers and sisters or even fraternal twins. We share a part of our identity with our twin. I do with Mary, just as Sam did with Seth. When Seth suddenly died last fall, I could not only see the pain that my sister was suffering, I could feel it. To the depths of my soul, I knew what she was going through, and I experienced it along with her. As I wept in my pain, Sam held me and comforted me as my loving husband. I knew that the most loving thing I could do for my sister was to share him with her and let him do the same for her.

"So, I did. I sent him over there several times a week to look after some household chore or some fabricated matter of Seth's estate. I attended endless ladies' prayer and sewing meetings—stitch and snitch' I call them—on weekday evenings to make his absence convenient. When he returned in the evening to our bed, I could smell her lavender perfume on his body, and it gave me a sense of warmth and love toward him, and I thanked God that I had been given such a gift of a loving and compassionate husband. As I said, Doctor Watson, I do not expect you to understand all of that, but it should not come as a complete shock to you if you have been reading your medical journals."

I had read some about some of these phenomena, but I had to ask about what I really could not comprehend.

"Speaking of God," I said, calmly but firmly, "what I fail to understand is how you justify what has taken place before Him. You are people of severe faith, and I do not believe that this type of behavior is allowed, regardless of the peculiarities of birth or of marriage."

She looked back at me and did not flinch. "God, in His wisdom, made me and Mary twins and did the same for Seth and Sam. So, as far as I am concerned, that is His problem to sort out. He can jolly well explain it to me when I get to heaven, and until that time, He will just have to live with it."

Inside my head, I was shaking my head in amazement. I did not have an opportunity to respond before Mrs. Cushing turned to the other part of our conversation.

"I can also tell you, Doctor, that no matter what your brilliant friend, Sherlock Holmes, has deduced, there is something that does not make sense about arresting Alec Fairbairn for the kidnapping and torture of my children."

"Would you mind, Mrs. Cushing, explaining what you just said?"

"I have known Alec all my life, first as a scholar in the same Sunday school and a member of the same church youth fellowship, and then for many years as my brother-in-law. He is greedy, wayward, foppish, worldly, angry, vindictive, and occasionally lazy. However, he is not a monster, and he could never do to my son and daughter what has been done to them. That, sir, does not make sense, and I cannot believe it."

I knew enough not to argue. I had seen enough during my war years, in my medical practice, and in my observation of scores of cases of Sherlock Holmes, to know that the most horrendously unbelievable things could be done by the least suspected of persons. I said no more and thanked this quite unusual lady for the tea. The man-servant let me out and hailed a cab.

I returned to Baker Street, expecting to be able then to go to my practice. There was, however, a note waiting for me from Holmes. It ran:

```
Fairbairn apprehended mid-morning at
Barings. On our way now to Scotland Yard.
If possible, please join us immediately.
```

Chapter Seven

The Wrong Right Man

t took about twenty-five minutes to get to the Yard building on the Embankment. I was ushered into Inspector Lestrade's office, where he and Holmes were sitting in silence. Holmes looked up at me as I entered.

"Our Mr. Fairbairn is clever enough to refuse to be interviewed without his lawyer being present and advising him. One has come over from the Middle Temple and is meeting with him now. They sent a note saying that they will be ready to talk in two minutes from now."

On schedule, a fellow, who I assumed to be a solicitor, entered, followed by a very nicely dressed and remarkably handsome gentleman of about forty-five years of age, who I assumed to be our culprit.

The lawyer opened the conversation. "Gentlemen, whatever evidence you have regarding charges of blackmail may be presented in court. I assure you that they will be challenged most vigorously. I fully expect that the case will be dismissed immediately. My much greater concern is the utterly slanderous and libelous false accusations that Mr. Sherlock Holmes has made against my client concerning the kidnapping and torture of the Cushing children. My client fervently denies any involvement or even any knowledge whatsoever of these matters. You have not a scrap of evidence linking him to this horrific crime, and I demand that you drop all these utterly baseless charges immediately. While you, Inspector, are protected by your position in Scotland Yard, I can promise, Mr. Sherlock Holmes, that you will be sued endlessly and forever until you are bankrupt and unable to ply your amateur trade anywhere in England, or the Empire, or even America. Is that understood, sir?"

Sherlock Holmes had been threatened more times by more lawyers than I could count. This blustering pettifogger was nothing new. Holmes ignored him completely and spoke directly to Alec Fairbairn.

"Where are the Cushing children, Mr. Fairbairn? You have taken them and are harming them, and I assure you that you will be spending the rest of your life in Newgate for doing so. And if you do not release them to us immediately, then I assure you that you will end your life on a gallows."

"How dare you threaten my client!" exploded the lawyer. Holmes continued to treat him as if he did not exist.

"Alec," he continued, "They are your niece and nephew. They have never done you any harm, ever."

"Mr. Holmes," said the accused in a puzzled tone, "I do not know what you are talking about. I know nothing whatsoever about

Sam's and Sarah's children other than what I have read in the papers. I thought they had run off to enjoy the fun things in life that all youth should be able to enjoy and to get out from under the fanatical yoke of religious oppression. What harm are you talking about?"

Here, Lestrade interrupted. He stood up and said, "Come with me please, Mr. Fairbairn, and bring your solicitor. Please follow me."

"Where are you taking us?" demanded the lawyer.

"To the basement. The morgue is down there."

We descended the stairs into a sub-basement and passed into the chilled unit in which bodies and, in our case, body parts were stored. We followed Lestrade over to a table that was covered with a cloth.

"Mr. Fairbairn," he said. "This is what I am talking about. These are the appendages of the Cushing children that we believe you have removed and sent to their parents."

In one long tug, he quickly removed the cloth, exposing the fingers, hands, feet, and forearms of Aaron and Miriam Cushing. He picked up one of the forearms and turned back to the accused and his lawyer, ready to wave it in their faces. The dramatic gesture was not necessary. I heard some anguished noises behind me and spun around in time to watch Alec Fairbairn drop to the floor in a faint, and the lawyer make a beeline to a hand basin by the door, into which he hurled his breakfast.

Holmes said nothing as we made our way back to Baker Street. Upon entering our parlor, he immediately lit up his pipe, sat in his chair, pulled his legs up underneath his body, and closed his eyes. I knew that he would remain in that position for hours as he went back over every detail we knew about this most horrible of cases and tried to put the disparate pieces together in his mind.

There was no point to any attempt on my part with conversation, so I changed my clothes and departed to attend to my medical practice.

I returned by suppertime. Holmes sat at the table and picked at his dinner, saying nothing. At ten o'clock in the evening, a knock came to the door. I descended the stairs and received a note from a page boy. It was addressed to Sherlock Holmes. He opened it, read it, and handed it to me. It ran:

```
Thank you for arresting the wrong man.
For a famous amateur detective, you most
certainly are stupid, stupid, stupid.
```

For want of something to say, I offered an observation.

"Is there any chance that one of Moriarty's minions could be behind this? It would be in their character to taunt you, would it not?"

He looked at me and, in a weary voice, replied, "Yes. Moriarty himself may be dead, but some of his web are still alive and active. And yes, it would be in keeping with their past actions to taunt me. But no, doctor, this is not his work. There is a tangle here that needs straightening out. Moriarty and his web of evildoers may have been enormously greedy for ill-gotten gain and power and respect from the criminal world, but they would never stoop so low as to torture children. And, so far, there is no motive, no demand for material gain, nothing other than the inflicting of incredible pain on the children and their parents. No, my friend, we are not up against a master criminal. We are doing battle with an utterly depraved, evil, vile man. Whoever is behind this is unlike any monster I have ever fought. And so far, he is winning."

He said no more, and I retired to bed. For the next three days, I filled my time with attending to my patients and forced myself to think of matters other than this horrible case. Late on the third evening, Lestrade came by to visit. He was likewise looking exhausted, and I knew that he had slept no more than had Holmes.

He entered and placed two more tarot cards on our table.

"*Temperance* and *The Sun*. Minus their left legs from the knee down. The box came with them. I had my men remove it before the family could look inside, but with the cards, they knew what it was. I am not sure how much longer they can bear up. I have placed one of our nurses in the home to keep watch. The mother is in such grief that I fear she might take her own life."

He walked over to the mantle and helped himself to a snifter and the bottle of brandy.

He sat down on the sofa, took and slow sip, and let out a weary sigh. "I don't know about you, Holmes, but in my thirty years in this business, I have never encountered anything so utterly diabolical. What can this devil possibly be wanting? What reason, then? If Fairbairn was not behind it with his blackmail demands, then who is?"

He looked at Holmes. For the past three decades, they had often been adversaries, never hesitating to give the other a competitive poke or take a strip off. Now they just looked at each other, both at a loss. It was if they were hoping against hope that the other might have some flash of insight, some spark of brilliance that would lead them out of the morass in which they were mired.

There was no such relief.

Holmes simply shook his head and said nothing.

"What," queried Lestrade, "happens next? How far will he go?"

"The next step will be horrible disfigurement of their young bodies, and, then, as a final painful indignity, he will murder them."

Lestrade sighed his forlorn agreement, rose, and departed.

Chapter Eight

The Press Learns All

XI

JUSTICE .

The next move was not what Holmes had predicted. It happened three days later, and I ran into it as soon as I opened the door on to Baker Street first thing in the morning while on my way to my practice. Four newsboys from four competing newspapers were shouting at the top of their lungs. All were screaming about the gruesome dismemberment of the Cushing children. Somehow the details of the story, which all the parties to it had kept under wraps, were now fully known to the press.

The responsible papers, of which we did have a small number, merely carried out factual reporting and gave the public the information about each letter, each tarot card, and each horrifying box delivered to the Cushings' house. The tabloids and even several of the broadsheets that had a sensationalist bent to their coverage expanded the stories with gut-wrenching speculative details about the slow and painful dismemberment process. The perceived screams of the young people as their fingers, hands, feet arms, and legs were slowly cut from their bodies were described in anguished colorful detail. Prints of the tarot cards were added to the stories with the appropriate appendages removed. Some went so far as to predict which body part would be subtracted from the victims next. I leave it to your imagination, as depraved and you can force it to be, to think on what parts they suggested.

That most depraved indignity to the human body that was predicted by the vermin in our tabloid press did, in fact, take place. Lestrade dropped by late in the evening several days later. He placed a single card on the table. It confirmed my worst possible fear. The card was *The Devil,* the fifteenth card of the Major Arcana. It depicts a young man and a young woman, both naked and chained around their necks and attached to the Devil. The young woman's breasts and young man's private parts had both been cut out.

"The box came to the house this evening," said Lestrade. "We were able to intercept it before the family could open it, but they saw the card, and they know what has taken place. The lady has taken to her bed with brain fever, and the father is bumbling around as if in an imbecilic daze. It is very hard on them. There was a note in the box. As cruel as you could imagine. Beyond imagining."

He placed the note on the table. It read:

```
No need to worry about blood loss.
Cauterizing with a hot iron cures
that.
```

"Any insights at all, Holmes? I confess, we are at a loss. Whoever is doing this must have some connection to either you or me, for he seems to know exactly what our moves have been. Anything?"

Holmes shook his head. "No, my friend, there is nothing. Nothing. We are simply not dealing with our standard criminal. Not even a diabolical, brilliant mind like Moriarty. This is a lone-wolf, and he is beyond evil and completely demented. I have not slept a wink, and it looks as you have not either. All we can do is keep going. Keep going over the evidence. Keep trying to put our heads inside that of a monster."

Lestrade shrugged his shoulders and rose and made his way to our door.

"I will catch up with you tomorrow. I have asked the morgue to have all of the boxes put out for me in the morning. I am going to look them over one more time. It is likely pointless, but you never know. You are welcome to join me."

"I will do that," said Holmes as Lestrade turned and descended our seventeen steps with a slow, heavy tread.

The following morning, I was again occupied with my patients, forcing myself one more time to direct my mind to anything other than this soul-destroying case. At ten o'clock, a page boy came bursting into my office and right into my examining room while I was checking over the prostrate body of an elderly woman. This was a terrible breach of rules and an embarrassing violation of the patient's privacy. I shouted at the lad to get out.

To his credit, he did not. "I'm sorry, doctor. I'm so sorry, but I was ordered to get this to you no matter what. I'm sorry. It's come from Scotland Yard. They said I had to get it to you and to interrupt you no matter what you were doing. Please, sir, I'm terrible sorry."

He handed me an envelope. As I opened it, the dear older lady who was lying prone on her stomach on my examining table rolled over, covered her sagging body with the sheet, and looked up.

"Owww, Scotland Yard, you say. Oh my, well that sounds a whole lot more fun than peering up me arse, don't it, Doc? Well, don't just stand there, boy, open it up, and let's see what you got."

I tore open the envelope. The note inside, scribbled hastily in Holmes's cramped handwriting, I read:

Come immediately to the morgue. Now! Break in Cushing case. COME IMMEDIATELY!

The dear woman had been looking over my shoulder as I read the note.

"Owww, Doc, you better get on your way. Don't you worry about me. Probably nothing wrong that a bowl of prunes won't fix. And don't I have a story now to tell all me old biddies. None of them ever had their doctor called away on the case in the headlines while bare-arsed on the table. Away you go, Doc."

I could not help smiling at her as I tore off my white coat and rushed out of the building. I stopped for just a few seconds to apologize to the patients sitting in my waiting room. The dear old patient's voice rang out from my the examination room as I did so.

"On your way, m'boy! Don't worry, I'll tell them all about it. Best story we'll have this week. Off you go!"

I leapt into a cab and shouted the destination to the cabbie. A smile appeared across his face, and he laid a whip on the back end of his horse, and we tore through the city. He quite seemed to enjoy being able to shout "Scotland Yard! Emergency!" repeatedly as we raced from Marylebone all the way to the Thames. I jumped out as soon as we arrived at the headquarters of the Yard, tossed the good fellow a sovereign, and ran into the building. The front desk was expecting me and immediately opened the doors down the stairwells to the morgue. I was huffing and puffing and sweating by the time I got to the room where Holmes and Lestrade were waiting for me.

"Merciful heavens, Holmes," I gasped while trying to catch my breath. "What in the world is it?"

"We need you, my friend," he replied. There was almost a touch of happiness appearing on his face. "You are the doctor, we are not. But come, please. Take a look at all of the body parts. Use my glass. We have also prepared several slides. They are by the microscope. Look at them too.

"What am I supposed to be looking for?"

"Just look, and tell us if you see the same thing we think we might have."

I looked first at the section of lower leg than had been severed from Miriam Cushing and then at the corresponding piece from her brother, Aaron. There was nothing unusual. Both were obviously limbs from young bodies that one might expect from athletic healthy people. I looked up, perplexed, at Holmes, and Lestrade. They just smiled.

"Just keep looking, Watson," said Lestrade.

I moved on to the young woman's breast. Something did not make sense. I went back to her leg and then back to the breast.

Now I was on fire. I went quickly over all of the parts. Then I looked at the slides that had been prepared for the microscope. After ten minutes, there was no need for further examination.

"These are not from the same body. There must be three young women's bodies and three of young men. The skins, at first, appear similar, but skin has a signature. None are exactly alike. These are different from each other in very subtle ways, but they are different. This is madness."

I could not imagine that a single madman had abducted at least six young people and was torturing them all. It made no sense whatsoever.

"Ah, thank you, Doctor," said Holmes. "It is what we thought but could not be sure. Thank you, my dear doctor."

"Can we really be dealing with someone so vile as to dismember six young people? Is that possible?" I was at a complete loss.

Holmes and Lestrade looked at each other and gave a respected nod one to the other.

"No doctor, I think not. Let us propose an alternative hypothesis. Are there any resurrectionists still active around London?"

The question set me back. In the earlier years of the nineteenth century, a trade had developed that called itself *resurrectionists*. They were more commonly known as body snatchers. Medical schools had been opening across the country, and there was a constant need of fresh cadavers for dissection and instruction in anatomy. For a number of years, all sorts of graves had been violated, but then the Anatomy Act had been passed, requiring licensing of medical schools, and that was supposed to have put an end to the trade.

"That is a good question," I said as I pondered an answer. "From time to time, we in the medical profession hear rumors of the sale of bodies and body parts, but no one has ever been arrested for it for years. No respectable, licensed medical school would be caught dead receiving cadavers from criminal sources."

"And," asked Lestrade, raising his eyebrows, "are all medical schools respectable and licensed?"

Most were, but of late, several privately-owned businesses had opened their doors and called themselves *Medical Instruction Centers.* They had been advertising heavily across the Empire and had accepted many students from Africa, India, and the Caribbean colonies. Whatever certificate they offered was not worth the paper it was printed on in Great Britain, Europe, or America. But it was deemed to be legitimate and indeed valued in many of our more primitive colonies.

"There are," I replied, "several independent operations that are not governed by the medical councils. Yes. There are a few around London."

"How big are they?" asked Holmes. "How many students might be enrolled?"

"I only know from hearsay," I said, unsure of myself. "There is one operating down in Croydon that is said to have over 500 students: the *Santo Christobel School of Medical Care.* They charge every one of their students upwards of £500 a year. Seems to be quite a profitable going concern."

"Are they licensed to receive cadavers from the hospitals or the prisons?" asked Lestrade.

"I would think not," I said. "That entire area is quite tightly controlled. It did not used to be, but now it is a felony to desecrate a corpse. Only approved institutions can receive cadavers for the teaching of anatomy."

"Well now, Holmes? Fancy a short trip down to Croydon?" asked Lestrade.

Holmes did not immediately reply, and then responded. "Yes, Inspector, but perhaps not in the daylight hours. If coffins and corpses are being transported around London, I presume it would be done after dark. Would you agree?"

"Right, that makes good sense, Holmes. So, what do you say? Meet up at dusk and pay a visit. Might not catch a delivery tonight, but I would wager we will snag one right soon. They must get them on a regular basis. I say we give it a try. Meet me at Victoria at seven this evening. I'll bring a couple of my bobbies along, just in case things get dicey."

"A capital idea," replied Holmes.

"And Holmes," continued Lestrade, "between now and then I am going home and having a jolly good nap. I suggest you do the same."

"The best idea you have had in years," replied Holmes, and, to the relief of both of them, they laughed.

In the cab on the way home, Holmes was more reflective. "I have disciplined myself not to jump to optimistic conclusions. It is always a dreadful temptation in this line of work. But my mind is suggesting quite strongly that the appendages that were delivered to the Cushing's home were not those of their children. There is a good chance that the youngsters are still alive and whole."

"Where?" I asked. It seemed to me to be the inevitable next question.

"I have no idea," he replied. "But one step at a time might lead us to them."

Chapter Nine

Resurrection Night

TEMPERANCE.

For the remainder of the day, I returned to my medical practice. My patients not only forgave me for making them wait for so long—many doctors do exactly the same thing all the time without offering any excuse at all, let alone being called for a command performance by Scotland Yard—they were all ears as soon as I returned, hoping for some juicy tidbit about the story that had so recently exploded on the public. I played coy and told them they would just have to wait.

At dusk, we reassembled at Victoria and boarded the LB&SCR south to the East Croydon station. Lestrade had organized a police carriage and a couple of bobbies who were prepared to spend the night with us, watching the back door of a questionable medical education institution.

The school was located on Cross Street, which was, quite fortunately, just a block from the station. With time to spare, we took a few minutes for a bite in the Dog and Bull. A plaque on the wall informed us that King Henry VIII had dined here, but with which of his wives beside him, it did not say. Once darkness had fallen, we walked across the tracks and found a couple of benches that gave us a good view of the back entrance to the school. The publican had sent along a sack with some meats, fruits, and rolls, and we chatted and nibbled for the next two hours. It was a warm late summer night, and the company was pleasant. Holmes and Lestrade were both now much more relaxed than they had been just yesterday, and the two young bobbies, Carl and Freddie, were jovial chaps who found any excuse possible for a round of laughter.

It was going on to eleven o'clock when Holmes laid his hand on my forearm and bid us all keep our voices down. In the dim light from the moon and a solitary gas lamp, we observed a livery wagon pulling up to the back door of the school. Lestrade rose and gestured to the rest of us.

"Follow me, please, gentlemen. Our plot appears to be unfolding."

From a vantage place alongside a hedgerow, we observed the back door of the school opening and three men emerging. Together with the liveryman, they lifted what were obviously coffins and carried four of them, one at a time, pallbearer style, into the building.

"Whatever the school is up to is not our concern this evening," whispered Holmes. "We need to learn the origin of the cadavers that have arrived here."

"Well now, sir," offered Freddie, "I think we can find that out right fast for you, sir. With your permission, Inspector, we'll just take a bit of a walk up to the driver and ask him, won't we Carl?"

Lestrade nodded his approval, and the two bobbies walked along the dark wall unseen until they were only a few feet from the wagon. One of the chaps from the school signed off on the delivery manifest and closed the door of the school. Carl and Freddie, doing what I assumed they had done many times before, were able to place themselves directly behind the driver, and the moment he turned around, he found himself staring right at them. Carl had his torch in hand and shone it directly in the poor fellow's face while Freddie barked commands at him. The driver staggered back and fell to the pavement, quite obviously scared out of his wits.

"Right," muttered Lestrade, "yet again, I get a couple of comedians. But let's go and chat with the man before he fills his boots."

"I were not doin' anythin' wrong, I weren't," he was sputtering to the bobbies. "This is a right legal and all delivery, I weren't disobeyin' any law."

"We will decide that, sir," said Lestrade in a firm voice. "Scotland Yard, here."

The look of panic on the chap's face was pitiable, but a bit funny all the same.

"All we need to know," said the inspector, "is who sent these coffins down here. It looks right suspicious coming in the middle of the night like this."

"They always sends them at night, they do, sir. A wagon with a pile of coffins goin' by gets all sorts of folks upset, especial when they can see that the wagon is loaded down so the coffins mustna be empty. I would a hae me a whole crowd of followers had I come in the daylight. This is just our common practice, sir."

"Is it now?" continued Lestrade. "Well, now, I do not find it common at all, so you might start by telling me where these came from. Getting rid of dead people in the middle of the night better have a good explanation."

"I come down from the river, sir. From the Thames, sir. To be specific, sir, from the Grosvenor Canal by the Chelsea Bridge, sir. Right beside the 'ospital, sir. Here sir, look at the manifest. It's right here, sir."

Freddie held his torch on the paper that was shaking in the fellow's hand. The sender was clearly identified. It read:

```
Grosvenor Marine Embalmers and
Undertakers, Gatliff Road,
Chelsea.
```

Lestrade and Holmes conferred for a few moments and then told the fellow to be on his way. He was much relieved.

"He will," said Holmes, "no doubt report his being accosted by Scotland Yard to the senders when he sees them tomorrow. If it is not too inconvenient to you, gentlemen, and as it is a pleasant evening, I suggest we continue our quest back along the Thames. We should be able to catch the late train back to Victoria. From there is a very short distance to the canal."

We returned to the station, boarded the 11:45 pm train back into London, and were on the platform of Victoria a half-hour later. It was a short few blocks south to the Grosvenor Canal, one of the many waterways that had been dug during the canal era and now was used primarily as a convenient place to load and unload barges from the Thames. It was lined by warehouse buildings, none of which looked like an undertaker's establishment. But, as the driver had told us, we found what we were looking for—a substantial brick building a half block from the Lister Institute.

I had, as a medical man, been in the Institute on several occasions in the past to listen to lectures by the renowned scientist, Sir Joseph Lister. Thanks to him, the practice of antiseptics had spread across the globe, saving untold thousands of lives. I had not, however, been aware of an undertaker's service adjacent to the famous institution.

It was now past midnight, and all of the doors were locked and the building closed for the night. It would not likely open much before seven in the morning if it was working on the same hours as the hospital. But that still meant we were faced with a wait of more hours than we wanted to spare. Holmes gave me a poke in the ribs and whispered in my ear.

"Isn't it time for your lunar lecture?" whispered Holmes.

I winked back at him.

"Now gentlemen," I said in a voice reserved for a public lecture, "do come with me and allow me to point out something that you have never, I assure you, seen before. Come this way. Now take a look up at the moon, nearly a full moon, is it not? Can you see the shaded spot on the upper left quadrant? That is not a crater, that is the eyeball of the man in the moon."

Lestrade and the bobbies had been following me out of curiosity up to that point. Now they looked at me as if I had gone completely barmy. The look did not last more than a second before Holmes called out to us.

"Oh, Look. The door is open, after all. They must still be doing business. How fortunate. Let us go in and find them."

Lestrade gave me a sharp look and strode up to Holmes, he was attempting to be officious, but his smile betrayed him.

"One of these days, Holmes, one of these days, you are going to get yourself in deep trouble doing things like that."

"What? Me? In trouble? Never, I am the most law-abiding consulting detective in London, I'll have you know."

"Right," muttered Lestrade, "and since you are the *only* consulting detective in London, that makes you also the least law-abiding."

He marched past Holmes and into the building. It did not take long for the bobbies to locate the light switches, and soon the hallways were fully illuminated. We followed Holmes down a stairwell to the basement, where he opened the door marked *Mortuary Cold Chambers*. A light switch was located just beside the door frame, and we found ourselves looking at a large sterile room where three walls were lined with the metal panels of morgue drawers. The room itself was chilly, and I could tell by looking at them that the glistening drawers were refrigerated. A few had frost on them, where bodies were completely frozen in order to prevent all decomposition. The remainder, and there were well over a hundred of them, were kept at a temperature just above freezing so that a corpse could be held for up to a month without any significant decomposition. A portion of the far wall consisted of much smaller morgue drawers than would be required for an adult man or woman. These, I realized, were for children.

"Crikey, what is this place?" whispered Freddie. "It's downright a bit creepy."

"Spooky, I'll say," added Carl. "Do all those drawers have dead folks in them?"

"Most of them, yes," said Holmes. "This is the establishment to which the bodies of those who die at seas are brought. Tens of thousands of children, men, and women, of all ages, board ships in Liverpool, Southampton, Portsmouth, or London on their way to the new world. Not all of them make it. Some invariably die on route. The shipping lines used to bury them at sea, but now they are brought back to England and, if there is family that can be contacted, they are returned for a decent burial. Those who cannot be placed are made available to our hospitals and medical schools so that their cadavers may be used in the teaching of anatomy."

"Right," said Lestrade. "Rather a sort of central cadaver supply depot."

"I suppose you could call it that, yes."

"Right then, Holmes. What are we looking for? Some young bodies that could pass for the Cushing children?"

"Exactly. There should be six or seven. Young adults. Fair skin. All minus an appendage or two. Most likely, they are grouped together, but that cannot be for certain. I suggest that we divide ourselves up and start pulling out morgue drawers."

We set ourselves to the task at hand. As a doctor, I had viewed countless corpses in the past, and looking at them was routine. Holmes, with his interest in forensics, had made many trips to the morgue, as had Lestrade in his years of service to the Yard. I suspected though that our two young bobbies had not likely been given an assignment like this before. I confess knowing that they should be warned that bumping the morgue drawers as you pulled them out occasionally released some tension in the chilled corpses, and they were known to move as the drawer was opened. But it was the middle of the night and a fine time for gallows humor, so I said nothing.

Carl and Freddie worked together at the far end of the room. They kept up a constant chatter between them, interspersed with nervous laughter. They were moving quickly, opening and closing drawers quite vigorously in their haste to finish the job. It was not long before one of them let out a scream of terror. I looked over and could see that a blue, naked body of an elderly man had sat up several inches, and one of his arms had sprung forward. Freddie had run back to the door of the room and was looking as if he had seen a ghost. I could not help laughing as I walked over to the opened drawer, put my hand on the old fellow's chest, pushed him back down, and closed up the drawer.

"You have to be gentle with these old folks, boys. They do not take kindly to being wakened up."

After some muttered oaths, the young bobbies went back to work. Some ten minutes later, they were laughing uproariously.

"What's the joke?" barked Lestrade. "You are expected to show respect for the dead. Now cut it out."

"Sorry, Inspector," said Carl. "It's just that we're assumin' that the fellows who run this place are dealin' some of the corpses out under the table, right? So, Freddie here had a good idea as to how to let them know that doing so wasn't on the up an' up. He could just lie down in one of these drawers and have a nap until the proprietors show up, and them when they pulls out his drawer he would sit right up and shout at them and say, 'I told you never to wake me up before ten. Now put me back!' Don't you think that would teach 'em a lesson, Inspector, sir?"

We all laughed, and we were still chuckling when Lestrade called out to us.

"Holmes, Watson, look here. There they are. I've just found three and ..." he continued to pull drawers open and leave them open as he spoke, "Yes. There's the fourth … and the fifth … and six."

We gathered around the six morgue drawers that were all exposed. In them were the bodies of three young men and three young women. The missing appendages all corresponded with the body parts that were stored in the police morgue at the Scotland Yard headquarters.

"Mark my words, Holmes," said Lestrade, "this is the first time in my thirty years with the Yard that I have been happy to see six dismembered corpses."

We stood briefly looking at the bodies of young men and women who had, not so long ago, boldly left their homes somewhere in old Europe and made their way to a new life across the ocean, only to succumb to accident, sickness, or possibly murder while at sea. Their remains were now destined to be dissected in the interests of medical education. I slowly closed up the morgue drawers, and the group of us turned out the lights prepared to depart the building.

"Constables," said Lestrade, "you remain here, and when the owners arrive, arrest them."

Freddie turned to Lestrade with a distraught look on his face. "Oh, Inspector, sir, you're not going to make us stay here all night, are you? Sir, you can send me after bank robbers who are holdin' a Gatlin gun, sir, but this place, sir, it's just unnatural, sir. I'm goin' to be seein' that blue grandpa sittin' up and lookin' at me every time I close my eyes, sir. Do we have to spend the night here?"

Lestrade laughed and gave the young bobby a clap on his shoulder. "No, I suppose not. The two of you can just keep walking around the neighborhood until dawn and then come back once the owners arrive in the morning and bring them down to the station. That will do."

"Oh, thank you, sir."

It was now just past two o'clock in the morning on one of the final nights of August. The weather was balmy, with a breeze blowing in off the river. The streets of London were empty, and it was almost pleasant to walk north back to Victoria Station. The relief we felt on confirming that the kidnapped children had not been inhumanly dismembered was palpable. Our work, however, was far from over.

"What happens, now?" I asked Holmes and Lestrade.

"The first thing," replied Holmes, "is to convey this news, very incomplete though it is, to the Cushing family. It will give them some relief from the pain and some basis for hope. Then we still have to find and rescue the children and try to make sense out of the monstrous and meaningless cruelty that has been inflicted on the family."

"There may," said Lestrade, wearily, "still be a ransom demand to come. This whole horrible series might just be the prolog."

We continued our walk in silence. Upon reaching Victoria Station, we were fortunate to find two cabs who were working through the night, and we parted ways with Lestrade. We came home and fell into our beds. I was fairly certain that it was the first decent sleep Holmes had allowed himself since this inexplicable case had begun two weeks ago.

Chapter Ten

We Did Not Get Ahead

DEATH.

rose well after eight o'clock the following morning. I was pleased to see that Holmes had not yet stirred, and I sat down quietly to enjoy my morning coffee. From the street, I could hear the newsboys peddling the morning papers, and I descended to Baker Street to get a copy. As I unfolded it and read the front page, my heart sank. The headline read:

HEADS OF CUSHING CHILDREN ARRIVE IN KNIGHTSBRIDGE

The story that followed went on to claim that the press had discovered that the final tarot card, *The Judgement,* had been delivered, with the heads of the male and female figures removed. Since the previous punctured cards had all been accompanied by the related body parts, it was assumed that the heads of the children had also been delivered. What followed was a repeating of the events of the past fortnight, fused with mindless speculations and nasty criticism of both Scotland Yard and Sherlock Holmes for failing to prevent this abominable crime of torture and murder.

"HOLMES!" I shouted at the door of his room. "You must come now!"

He emerged in his dressing gown, took one look at the newspaper I held in front of him, and immediately returned to his bedchamber to bathe and dress. Ten minutes later, we were in a cab and on our way to Knightsbridge.

"What are you going to say to the Cushings?" I asked him.

"I will tell them what we know, and no more and no less."

"And just what is it that we now know?"

"Oh, come, come, my good doctor. You know perfectly well what we know. We know that the body parts they received are not from their children and that they were taken from a morgue. And that is all we know for certain. We do not know where their children are nor why they have been kidnapped, nor why no ransom note has been received from the true kidnapper. And we have no idea who is behind this monstrous and cruel hoax. That is what we know and what we do not."

"Is it permissible to offer them hope?"

"They will grasp all possible hope without any assistance from us. We will also make a promise to them not to rest until their children are returned to them safely. I believe I will be on safe grounds in making that same promise on behalf of Inspector Lestrade. Would you agree?"

"Yes. Yes. That all seems quite in order."

As we turned onto the block of Ennismore Gardens in which the Cushing family lived, I looked up the street and inwardly groaned. There was a large gaggle of reporters gathered in front of the house. Two of Lestrade's constables were keeping them back from the doors and windows, but there was no possible way we could enter the house without running their gantlet. I chanced to look behind our cab and noticed a Scotland Yard carriage following us. The good inspector had clearly had the same compulsion to come immediately to the family's home and relieve them of the latest agony that the kidnapper and the press had inflicted on them.

Lestrade and Holmes exited their carriages at the same moment and were immediately swarmed by the press. Although we ignored them, it was impossible not to be cut by the jibes and insults.

"Halloo, Sherlock Holmes. How did the kidnapper get *A…HEAD* of you?" Raucous laughter followed.

"Hey there, Inspector. What will Scotland Yard put on the gravestones? How about *REST IN PIECES!*"

"Are you going to ask the corpses to *GIVE YOU A HAND?*" This was deemed oh-so-clever, and there was a round of self-congratulatory back-slapping. More taunts followed until we entered the house. The man-servant, Mr. Browner, led us into the parlor. He stood at attention and bid us be seated.

"I'm dreadfully sorry, gentlemen. The master and mistress are in the library, along with some of the elders from the Assembly. They are having a time of prayer. I do not expect they will be much longer. May I bring you some coffee and some pastries while you wait?"

"Good heavens, man," snapped Lestrade. "Just go and interrupt them and tell them to get in here. This is much more important, and I am sure God will not object."

"Yes, sir. Of course, sir. I will interrupt as soon as the current participant has finished his prayer. But do be patient, they tend to go a long time."

He clicked his heels again and retreated to the back of the house.

It was a full ten minutes before a small troop of prayer warriors emerged from the library and joined us in the parlor. Mrs. Cushing was with them, supported on the arm of one of the saintly sisters. Samuel Cushing brought up the rear and looked as physically drained as I had ever seen a man who was still on his feet and walking forward.

They apparently had all decided to be part of our disclosures and took chairs around the sides of the spacious parlor. Once Mr. Cushing had seated himself beside his wife on the sofa, I could see that Inspector Lestrade was ready to take command of the meeting. He did not speak up quickly enough. One of the gentlemen from the church announced that the gathering would begin with prayer, and he stood and began to deliver. Being a somewhat less-than-regular adherent of the Catholic faith, I was not used to prayers that lasted more than a minute. Now I sat and listened while the good Lord above was reminded of more verses of Scripture than I could have imagined could have been called upon in such a time of need. I confess that I had always thought the Heavenly Father, having dictated all those verses Himself, knew all those passages quite well and needed no reminders. If that were not enough, the dear saintly elder kept blessing the now-departed souls of the dead children and gave a favorable report of their current joy as they walked the streets of gold. And finally, he managed to come up with a memory verse that was connected in some way to the various parts of the bodies that had been detached and shipped through the local livery service. A postscript was added beseeching divine guidance for both Sherlock Holmes and Inspector Lestrade who, it was to be concluded, were obviously in desperate need of same.

With the exception of Holmes, Lestrade and me, all others in the room kept their heads bowed and their eyes tightly shut. The three of us kept peering at each other in silence, rolling our eyes, shrugging our shoulders, and waiting until the heavens put the dear brother on hold and let us say our piece. Finally, he ended, and a round of audible *amens* was added by the other elders present.

Lestrade seized the opportunity, and in a firm, confident voice announced, "Please, all of you, give me your attention. The various body parts that have been delivered to the Cushing family are absolutely and most certainly NOT from the bodies of young Aaron and Miriam Cushing. They were illegally taken from bodies in a morgue and used to falsely represent appendages of the children. This we know for certain. Those who defiled the corpses have been arrested, and this cruel charade has been stopped. No heads from any bodies have been delivered, and we are certain that no heads ever will be delivered.

"At this time, the investigation is receiving all available help from Scotland Yard as well as the services of Mr. Sherlock Holmes. We do not yet know where the children are, nor who has taken them, nor what sort of ransom will be demanded, nor why this monstrous hoax has been played out. However, we will continue to work around the clock to answer all of those questions, and our first priority will be the safe return of the children to their families.

"Now, Scotland Yard needs to ask further questions of the family, and so I am directing all of you, except members of the Cushing household, on the authority of His Majesty's national police force, to vacate these premises immediately so that our investigation may proceed. Thank you for your generous and compassionate assistance to the family. Now, please, all of you, be on your way. Thank you."

One of the sainted brethren objected. "I beg to inform you, Inspector, that we have had word from the Lord that we should be here and …"

Lestrade was having none of that and cut him off. "Unfortunately, sir, the Lord has not yet got around to sending that word to me, and since this is now police business, I am the one He has to inform. So kindly do as I have requested and vacate the premises, thank you. Your assistance to the family is appreciated."

He rose as he spoke, moved to the entrance to the parlor, and gestured toward the door. The saints from the Assembly, somewhat begrudgingly perhaps, rose and left the house. From a gap in the curtains, I could see the press descend upon them like hungry locusts. I was sure that they would repeat to the press what they had been told by the inspector, and that the news would appear in the next available edition of the day's newspapers.

The man-servant appeared with yet another round of coffee, tea, and sweetbreads. We partook while Lestrade slowly and patiently repeated questions that had been posed earlier to the family, seeking to unearth whoever had both a close connection to the household and might harbor such venomous hatred toward them.

Samuel Cushing kept going back over his life and career. Yet no credible suspect emerged. "I have had," he said, "strong disagreements with many senior men in Whitehall and many elected representatives in Westminster. But there was no one, not a one, who was not an honorable gentleman, who would take it upon himself to act in such an evil manner. Not a one, sir."

When Lestrade had shot his bolt and come up empty, Holmes took over and directed his questions, firmly but gently toward both Mr. and Mrs. Cushing. His queries were politely stated but went right to the very depths of their private lives.

"Forgive me," he said, "but we can leave no stone unturned. I assure you that whatever you say to us will be held in the strictest confidence, but I fear I must ask you some questions, and the answers may be painfully private."

The two Cushings looked at each other, nodded, then turned and nodded to Holmes. I made a point of closing up my notebook and putting it back in my pocket.

Over the next hour, he probed all aspects of Mr. Cushing's career in the Foreign Service, his friendship and possible conflicts within his church and the affiliated Assemblies, his purchases of properties or securities, and his dealings with the schoolmasters of his children. All of these areas, Holmes had learned, were fertile ground for deeply held conflicts between and among people. He then turned to Mrs. Cushing and did the same. She gave forthright answers about her friends within the church and those with whom she had tangled, about her hiring and firing of domestic help, about her dealings with local councils, neighbors, dustmen, grocers, and the like. Again, she clearly held nothing back and admitted to occasions when her temper had gotten the better of her. There had been the odd spot of friction, which was not surprising given her strong-willed character, but nothing that could conceivably invoke the cruel animosity to which they had been subjected.

Finally, Holmes went directly to the matter of the confession that Mr. Cushing had made over a week ago. The man blushed with shame as he recounted it in front of his wife. She never stopped looking up at him in love and adoration, although he was not looking back at her. She slowly slid her hand forward until it was against his and interlaced their fingers. I could see her knuckles whiten slightly as she applied pressure against his fingers. He turned and looked into her face, and she whispered, "Darling, I know. And I love you all the more."

Yet again, without visibly appearing to do so, I was mentally shaking my head. There were some things I would never understand. Lestrade, who had not been privy to the earlier conversation between Holmes and Samuel Cushing, was speechless and rendered positively bug-eyed.

Finally, Holmes looked directly at Mrs. Cushing and asked if she had ever had a lover.

She first looked up at her husband, smiled warmly, and then replied to Holmes.

"Yes…and no. It would not be accurate to call him a lover."

Her husband's eyes nearly popped from his head.

She smiled back. "When my sister was in her final month of pregnancy, and then during the first month after giving birth to her son, she was in no mood whatsoever for physical intimacy with Seth. She and I knew that both Seth and Sam had been blessed with powerful animal spirits of which we were the fortunate beneficiaries, but we also knew that the time when a young husband is most likely to stray was during those months when his wife was not looking after his needs. So, we chatted about it, and for a period of about two months, I agreed to pretend to be her and make sure that Seth was duly exhausted on a regular basis."

"And did your sister," Holmes asked, "reciprocate during your pregnancies?"

"Oh, no. It was not necessary. My husband followed the advice that is given to all men by their doctors during that time of their lives. You know—*if you wife cannot be your right hand, let your right hand be your wife.*"

Sam Cushing looked at his wife in disbelief. "You knew … you *knew* I was doing that?"

"Well, of course, darling. You were not exactly quiet about it."

I could see Lestrade becoming progressively less comfortable, and he began to squirm in his chair. Holmes finally wound down his questions, and the five of us sat back in our chairs, emotionally exhausted. This devout couple who sat in front of us had bared the most intimate details of the souls to us and to each other. Tears were running freely down Mrs. Cushing's face, and she had placed both hands around her husband's arms and was clinging tightly.

I shot a quick glance out the window and was relieved to see that the press had departed, required no doubt to run back to Fleet Street to file their stories about the body parts from the morgue. Our path out and into Lestrade's police carriage would be mercifully unobstructed.

While I was looking, Holmes and Lestrade were concluding the interview and going over a few of the answers they had received to make certain that they had understood everything correctly.

We were loudly interrupted.

The front door of the house opened, followed by a clatter and banging, and then the slamming of it shut again. And then a shout.

"Haaaalloooo!! We're hoooome!!!"

THE DEVIL .

Chapter Eleven

Kidnapped to Guernsey

THE SUN .

After a few more bumps, bangs and crashes two young people burst into the parlor.

"Oh, Daddy," bubbled the young woman, "it was absolutely brilliant. Thank you sooo much. We had a wonderful time. It was the best, Daddy. Thank you."

The slender, tanned youngster threw herself forward toward Mr. Cushing, flung her arms around him, and gave him a large, noisy kiss on the cheek.

"Muuuaaahhh!" she added a sound to her kiss. She then turned to face Mrs. Cushing and repeated the affectionate act.

Immediately behind her came a tall, fine-looking young man. Like his sister, he was casually but smartly dressed, tanned, and beaming with a smile from ear to ear.

"Dad, thanks. That was the best surprise we could ever imagine. It was great."

Here he stopped, suddenly becoming aware that there were three strangers in his parlor.

"Oh, oh. I'm sorry. Are you having a meeting? Oh, sorry. We'll be on our way. But we just had to tell you, thank you. It was bang up the elephant. There were fellows and girls from all over Europe and America. Miri and I have never had such a good time."

"Oh, my, didn't we though," exclaimed the young woman. "You should have seen how well we did. You would be sooo proud of us. My brother won the harrier race. He won, Mommy, doesn't that just take the egg! There were boys from all over the place, and he won. I was sooo proud of him."

"Ahh, it wasn't all that special" returned the young man. "Some of the Swiss boys could run, but the rest of them, the French and the Italians, they may as well of had no feet and been running on their stumps. But you should have seen Miriam. She took two prizes. She won the girls swim and the girls hundred-yard dash. Of course, they wouldn't let the boys watch up close, but I could tell it was her. She won two trophies. You must show them to Momsy and Dad, Sis. Go get them!"

"Oh, good idea. Sorry, I know we're disturbing your meeting. But I just have to show them to you. Can we put them on the mantle, Daddy? Just wait, I'll be right back."

She dashed out of the room, grabbing her suitcase as she entered the hall, and I could hear the loud thumps of her ascending the stairs, two at a time.

"Oh, and Dad," rattled on the lad. "It wasn't all just fun and games and a big benjo. The speakers were really top-drawer, especially the chap from Georgia, in America. We poked a bit of fun at the way he talked but, whoa, could he preach. And Dad, you'll be sooo proud of Miriam and me. They put us on the same Bible Quiz team. She didn't like that at all because she was quite taken with Jeremy, from Edinburgh and wanted to be on his team ..."

"And you," came a voice from the second floor, "were pretty sweet on Tabitha, your cute little chica bonita from Madrid."

The whirlwind did not let up. There had not been a chance for a single word from one of the adults present. The young man blushed and shrugged his shoulders. "Oh, yes, well, her. But on the Bible quiz, they put Miri and me on the same team, and dad, we killed them. Quite knocked the blocks off the other teams. They gave us both brand new Scofield Bibles as prizes.

"Mommy?... Daddy?" came the voice from up the stairs again. "What are these doing on my dresser?"

She came back into the room wearing a very perplexed look on her face and holding in her hands two envelopes.

"These were on my dresser. One is a letter to you, Daddy. The other is addressed to...to Mr. Sherlock Holmes."

Holmes immediately stood up and approached the young woman. "I am Sherlock Holmes. You may give that letter to me."

The lad immediately jolted around and stared at Holmes. "*You* are Sherlock Holmes? In *our* house? Sherlock Holmes is in our house? That ... that takes the biscuit. Daaaad? Are you helping Sherlock Holmes solve one of his mysteries? Is that why the two mutton-shankers were standing out on the pavement? That's the best yet. Gosh, Mr. Holmes, this takes the Huntley. All my friends have read all your stories. Michaelmas starts next week. That will be so spot on for me to be able to tell them that my father is helping

Sherlock Holmes. Gosh, Dad, you really are full of surprises this summer. We thought we were going to be in morbs all month with you not letting us go to Guernsey for the youth conference, and then at the last minute, you did, and now we come home, and you're helping Sherlock Holmes."

He walked over to his father, who was still seated and had yet to say anything, and playfully put his hand on his father's forehead.

"Are you feeling all right, Dad? Did something happen, Momsy, when dad turned fifty?" He laughed playfully.

Then he looked back at Lestrade and me. "Are you Dr. Watson? And, you, sir, why you must be Inspector Lestrade. Oh, this is absolutely tooo much. Oh, I'm sorry this must be an important meeting we've interrupted. Let's go, Sis, race you to the loo."

With that, the young man and young woman crashed and stomped and laughed on the way up the stairs, and five adults were left in the parlor, completely walloped.

O

THE FOOL.

94

Chapter Twelve

This Circle of Misery

THE HANGED MAN.

Mr. Cushing opened the letter addressed to him, and Holmes did likewise. Inserted into Mr. Cushing's letter was a tarot card –*The Tower*, in flames, with bodies falling from it. Inserted into Holmes's card was *The Fool*.

The letter to Mr. Samuel Cushing. With copy to Mr. Sherlock Holmes:

By the time you read this, you will have known for a mere three weeks something of the pain and suffering that I, my sister, and my mother have endured for the past thirty years –

all because of you, Mr. Samuel
Cushing.

In 1884, my father was a brave and
loyal young officer in the B.E.F. and
proudly serving under one of our
country's most heroic leaders, General
Charles Gordon. My father belonged to
the regiment of courageous men who
defended the garrison and loyal
subjects in Khartoum. He sent letters
back to us, assuring us that
reinforcements were on their way and
that he would soon be home, safe and
sound.

Those reinforcements never arrived.
My father died on the night of 25
January 1885 when the city he and his
fellow soldiers was defending was
besieged by the Mahdi. The
reinforcements arrived two days later.

Do you know how my father died, Mr.
Cushing? He was tortured. One by one,
his fingers, his hands, his feet, his
arms, his legs, and his genitals were
cut off. Finally, they cut off his
head. When his coffin arrived back in
England two months later, no one

warned us not to open it and bid our
final respects to a brave man and
wonderful loving husband and father.
Inside the coffin were the various
parts of his body, in no order. His
severed head was looking up at us from
the middle of the box. I have never
been able to get the terror of that
moment to leave my mind. My dear
mother went partially mad. She lived
out her life on a meager widow's
pension, cared for by the saints of
the Methodist Church. My sister was
disturbed for years, finally pulling
her wits back together and marrying a
widower when she was past forty. She
now lives in some god-forsaken corner
of Canada, where I can only hope that
the freezing temperatures have numbed
her memory.

For my part, in honor of my father,
I joined the B.E.F. and have served
proudly all over the world. Every time
I returned to England, I did some more
research and sought to learn just what
had happened at Khartoum and why an
entire regiment and ten thousand
inhabitants of the city who were loyal
to the Queen were allowed to be

slaughtered. At first, I put the blame on Gladstone, but as I learned more, I understood that he and his cabinet acted on the advice and information provided to them by their mandarins in the Foreign Office. The oh-so-brilliant Cambridge man who had the Egypt-Sudan desk was named Samuel Cushing.

It was you, Mr. Cushing, that gave false and misleading information to the Cabinet. It was you who was responsible for the horrible death of my father and the destruction of my family.

When I retired from the B.E.F., I determined that somehow I would avenge the death of my father, and I watched your home constantly. I saw how you had prospered, and risen at Whitehall, and become so respected as a Christian. As far as I am concerned, you are no more than a whited sepulcher.

I befriended your former man-servant and learned of your so-called ministry given to the household help.

It was an easy thing to feign drunkenness and stroll into your gospel meeting and then to profess salvation through your fanatical faith. And so, you hired me as your butler.

I watched you for days and soon discovered your adulterous relationship with your sister-in-law. You wretched hypocrite. You who stand up every Sunday morning and lead in prayer for the bread and the wine. You are a lecher, and the world should know. Unfortunately, your foolish brother-in-law, Fairbairn, was greedy and stupid and used the information I gave him to blackmail you instead of exposing your hypocrisy to the world.

Undeserving though you are, you were blessed with exceptional children, and it was not difficult to gain their confidence. All spring and summer they begged you to let them attend the European Conference for Christian Youth that was to be held in August on the Island of Guernsey. You refused on some nonsensical ground of not wanting them to be unequally yoked

with those who were not your special
type of believers.

So, I sent in their registrations
and intercepted the confirmations. I
made the travel arrangements, and when
they were returning from their Bible
study, I drove up to them, their bags
packed and announced that you had had
a change of heart and had agreed to
let them go. They were over the moon.
But we had to rush. We sped to
Victoria and from there to Portsmouth.
By the time you were searching
Kensington Gardens, they were on the
night ferry across the Channel.

And then, Mr. Cushing, for the next
three weeks, you had a taste of what
I, my sister, and my mother endured.
You could feel the horror, the pain,
the agony in your heart of knowing
that those members of your family,
those you loved so dearly, were being
horribly tortured and put to death.

The appendages you received were
not from your children, as you now
know. They were, as Sherlock Holmes
and Scotland Yard finally deduced,

from bodies of young men and women who had already died and whose cadavers could be bought for a few quid under the table.

Now you have your children back. You are lucky. My father never returned, except in pieces. Now you can put your brief time of agony behind you. We never will.

By the time you read this, I will have departed England and be on the high seas.

Do not bother trying to find a Mr. Jim Browner.

He does not exist.

Lestrade and I had been reading over Holmes's shoulder. Mrs. Cushing had been doing the same over her husband's. We all finished reading at the same time and looked up at each other. Without speaking, Holmes, Lestrade, and I rose and prepared to leave the room. I stepped over to Samuel Cushing and shook his hand. Lestrade and Holmes did not.

That evening marked the arrival of the cool evenings of the late summer. Holmes and I sat by the hearth, lit for the first time since the spring. Holmes took the letter from his suit pocket and read it, and read it again.

"What is the meaning of it, Watson?" said Holmes solemnly as he laid down the paper. "What object is served by this circle of misery and violence and fear? It must tend to some end, or else our universe is ruled by chance, which is unthinkable. But what end? There is the great standing perennial problem to which human reason is as far from an answer as ever."

Did you enjoy this story? Are there ways it could have been improved? Please help the author and future readers of future New Sherlock Holmes Mysteries by posting a review on the site from which you purchased this book. Thanks, and happy sleuthing and deducing.

Dear Sherlockian Reader:

If you are familiar with the publication of the stories in The Canon, you will recall that Arthur Conan Doyle restricted the publication of *The Adventure of the Cardboard Box* for many years as he thought the subject matter was not suitable for reading by boys. Given that he pushed the boundaries of his time, I felt somewhat free to do likewise with a 21st Century pastiche story that contained similar themes. Hope you didn't mind.

When doing research for the story, I learned many more things about the late Victorian/Edwardian era. Here is some of what I came across that I thought might be of interest to you.

The Russo-Japanese War took place in 1904–1905. The Japanese soundly defeated the Russians. The ownership of a few islands that are part of the archipelago between Hokkaido and Kamchatka is still disputed.

Tarot Cards emerged as a set of playing cards in fifteenth-century Europe. The were adopted by occultists for use in divination in the eighteenth century and are still used widely for that purpose. The Rider Waite edition of the cards, designed by illustrator Pamela Coleman Smith, was created in 1909 and has been the most popular version of the cards since that time. In this story, *The Box of Cards,* the date of publication has been advanced.

The violation of fresh graves for the purpose of procuring cadavers for anatomy classes was quite common during the first half of the nineteenth century. The practice was curtailed by the Anatomy Act, but sporadic incidences took place for many decades afterward. The morgue for bodies of those who die at sea is fictional.

The Siege of Khartoun began in March 1884. Prime Minister Gladstone had decided to abandon the city along with the Sudan.

General Charles ("Chinese") Gordon refused to do so, knowing that the enemies would slaughter the non-British inhabitants who had been loyal to the Empire. You can read about the siege and the death of Gordon online or in many history books.

In the original Sherlock Holmes story, *The Adventure of the Cardboard Box*, Watson refers to the picture of *The Death of General Gordon*. It was that reference that inspired the connection in this new mystery.

The Darbyites were a branch of the Plymouth Brethren movement, and they, along with other branches of the Brethren Assemblies, are still to be found throughout the world. I grew up in this sect, and while I am no longer a part of them, many of the good people I met in those years still have my utmost respect.

References to locations, roads, buildings and institutions in London in 1905 are generally accurate.

Thank you for reading this tribute story. Hope you enjoyed it.

Warm regards,

Craig

About the Author

In May of 2014 the Sherlock Holmes Society of Canada – better known as The Bootmakers (www.torontobootmakers.com) – announced a contest for a new Sherlock Holmes story. Although he had no experience writing fiction, the author, Craig Stephen Copland, submitted a short Sherlock Holmes mystery and was blessed to be declared one of the winners. Thus inspired, he has continued to write new Sherlock Holmes mysteries since and is on a quest to write a new mystery that is inspired by each of the sixty stories in the original Canon. He has been writing from Toronto, Tokyo, Manhattan, Buenos Aires, Bahrain and the Okanagan Valley.. More about him and contact information can be found at

www.SherlockHolmesMystery.com.

New Sherlock Holmes Mysteries
by Craig Stephen Copland

www.SherlockHolmesMystery.com

"Best selling series of new Sherlock Holmes stories. All faithful to The Canon."

This is the first book in the series. Go to my website, start with this one and enjoy MORE SHERLOCK.

Studying Scarlet. Starlet O'Halloran, a fabulous mature woman, who reminds the reader of Scarlet O'Hara (but who, for copyright reasons cannot actually be her) has arrived in London looking for her long-lost husband, Brett (who resembles Rhett Butler, but who, for copyright reasons, cannot actually be him). She enlists the help of Sherlock Holmes. This is an unauthorized parody, inspired by Arthur Conan Doyle's *A Study in Scarlet* and Margaret Mitchell's *Gone with the Wind*.

Six new Sherlock Holmes stories are always free to enjoy. If you have not already read them, go to this site, sign up, download and enjoy. www.SherlockHolmesMystery.com

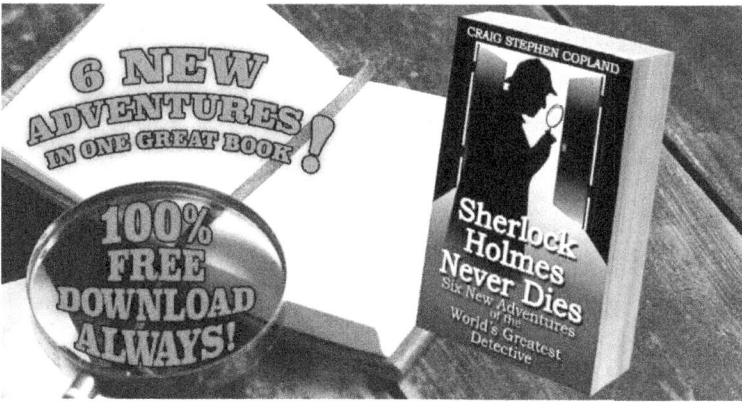

Super Collections A, B and C

57 New Sherlock Holmes Mysteries.

The perfect ebooks for readers who subscribe to Kindle Unlimited

Enter 'Craig Stephen Copland Sherlock Holmes Super Collection' into your Amazon search bar. Enjoy over 2 million words of MORE SHERLOCK.

www.SherlockHolmesMystery.com

The Adventure of the Cardboard Box

The Original Sherlock Holmes
Story

Arthur Conan Doyle

The Adventure of the Cardboard Box

In choosing a few typical cases which illustrate the remarkable mental qualities of my friend, Sherlock Holmes, I have endeavoured, as far as possible, to select those which presented the minimum of sensationalism, while offering a fair field for his talents. It is, however, unfortunately impossible entirely to separate the sensational from the criminal, and a chronicler is left in the dilemma that he must either sacrifice details which are essential to his statement and so give a false impression of the problem, or he must use matter which chance, and not choice, has provided him with. With this short preface I shall turn to my notes of what proved to be a strange, though a peculiarly terrible, chain of events.

It was a blazing hot day in August. Baker Street was like an oven, and the glare of the sunlight upon the yellow brickwork of the house across the road was painful to the eye. It was hard to believe that these were the same walls which loomed so gloomily through the fogs of winter. Our blinds were half-drawn, and Holmes lay curled upon the sofa, reading and re-reading a letter which he had received by the morning post. For myself, my term of service in India had trained me to stand heat better than cold, and a thermometer at ninety was no hardship. But the morning paper was uninteresting. Parliament had risen. Everybody was out of town, and I yearned for the glades of the New Forest or the shingle of Southsea. A depleted bank account had caused me to postpone my holiday, and as to my companion, neither the country nor the sea presented the slightest attraction to him. He loved to lie in the very center of five millions of people, with his filaments stretching out and running through them, responsive to every little rumour or suspicion of unsolved crime. Appreciation of nature found no place among his many gifts, and his only change was when he turned his mind from the evil-doer of the town to track down his brother of the country.

Finding that Holmes was too absorbed for conversation I had tossed side the barren paper, and leaning back in my chair I fell into a brown study. Suddenly my companion's voice broke in upon my thoughts:

"You are right, Watson," said he. "It does seem a most preposterous way of settling a dispute."

"Most preposterous!" I exclaimed, and then suddenly realizing how he had echoed the inmost thought of my soul, I sat up in my chair and stared at him in blank amazement.

"What is this, Holmes?" I cried. "This is beyond anything which I could have imagined."

He laughed heartily at my perplexity.

"You remember," said he, "that some little time ago when I read you the passage in one of Poe's sketches in which a close reasoner follows the unspoken thoughts of his companion, you were inclined to treat the matter as a mere tour-de-force of the author. On my remarking that I was constantly in the habit of doing the same thing you expressed incredulity."

"Oh, no!"

"Perhaps not with your tongue, my dear Watson, but certainly with your eyebrows. So when I saw you throw down your paper and enter upon a train of thought, I was very happy to have the opportunity of reading it off, and eventually of breaking into it, as a proof that I had been in rapport with you."

But I was still far from satisfied. "In the example which you read to me," said I, "the reasoner drew his conclusions from the actions of the man whom he observed. If I remember right, he stumbled over a heap of stones, looked up at the stars, and so on. But I have been seated quietly in my chair, and what clues can I have given you?"

"You do yourself an injustice. The features are given to man as the means by which he shall express his emotions, and yours are faithful servants."

"Do you mean to say that you read my train of thoughts from my features?"

"Your features and especially your eyes. Perhaps you cannot yourself recall how your reverie commenced?"

"No, I cannot."

"Then I will tell you. After throwing down your paper, which was the action which drew my attention to you, you sat for half a minute with a vacant expression. Then your eyes fixed themselves upon your newly framed picture of General Gordon, and I saw by the alteration in your face that a train of thought had been started. But it did not lead very far. Your eyes flashed across to the unframed portrait of Henry Ward Beecher which stands upon the top of your books. Then you glanced up at the wall, and of course your meaning was obvious. You were thinking that if the portrait were framed it would just cover that bare space and correspond with Gordon's picture there."

"You have followed me wonderfully!" I exclaimed.

"So far I could hardly have gone astray. But now your thoughts went back to Beecher, and you looked hard across as if you were studying the character in his features. Then your eyes ceased to pucker, but you continued to look across, and your face was thoughtful. You were recalling the incidents of Beecher's career. I was well aware that you could not do this without thinking of the mission which he undertook on behalf of the North at the time of the Civil War, for I remember your expressing your passionate indignation at the way in which he was received by the more turbulent of our people. You felt so strongly about it that I knew you could not think of Beecher without thinking of that also. When a moment later I saw your eyes wander away from the picture, I suspected that your mind had now turned to the Civil War, and when I observed that your lips set, your eyes sparkled, and your hands clenched I was positive that you were indeed thinking of the gallantry which was shown by both sides in that desperate struggle. But then, again, your face grew sadder, you shook your head. You were dwelling upon the sadness and horror and useless waste of life. Your hand stole towards your own old wound and a smile quivered on your lips, which showed me that the ridiculous side of this method of settling international questions had forced itself upon your mind. At this point I agreed with you that it was preposterous and was glad to find that all my deductions had been correct."

"Absolutely!" said I. "And now that you have explained it, I confess that I am as amazed as before."

"It was very superficial, my dear Watson, I assure you. I should not have intruded it upon your attention had you not shown some incredulity the other day. But I have in my hands here a little problem which may prove to be more difficult of solution than my small essay I thought reading. Have you observed in the paper a short paragraph referring to the remarkable contents of a packet sent through the post to Miss Cushing, of Cross Street, Croydon?"

"No, I saw nothing."

"Ah! then you must have overlooked it. Just toss it over to me. Here it is, under the financial column. Perhaps you would be good enough to read it aloud."

I picked up the paper which he had thrown back to me and read the paragraph indicated. It was headed, "A Gruesome Packet."

"Miss Susan Cushing, living at Cross Street, Croydon, has been made the victim of what must be regarded as a peculiarly revolting practical joke unless some more sinister meaning should prove to be attached to the incident. At two o'clock yesterday afternoon a small packet, wrapped in brown paper, was handed in by the postman. A cardboard box was inside, which was filled with coarse salt. On emptying this, Miss Cushing was horrified to find two human ears, apparently quite freshly severed. The box had been sent by parcel post from Belfast upon the morning before. There is no indication as to the sender, and the matter is the more mysterious as Miss Cushing, who is a maiden lady of fifty, has led a most retired life, and has so few acquaintances or correspondents that it is a rare event for her to receive anything through the post. Some years ago, however, when she resided at Penge, she let apartments in her house to three young medical students, whom she was obliged to get rid of on account of their noisy and irregular habits. The police are of opinion that this outrage may have been perpetrated upon Miss Cushing by these youths, who owed her a grudge and who hoped to frighten her by sending her these relics of the dissecting-rooms. Some probability is lent to the theory by the fact that one of these students came from the north of Ireland, and, to the best of Miss Cushing's belief, from Belfast. In the meantime, the matter is being actively investigated, Mr. Lestrade, one of the very smartest of our detective officers, being in charge of the case."

"So much for the Daily Chronicle," said Holmes as I finished reading. "Now for our friend Lestrade. I had a note from him this morning, in which he says:

"I think that this case is very much in your line. We have every hope of clearing the matter up, but we find a little difficulty in getting anything to work upon. We have, of course, wired to the Belfast post-office, but a large number of parcels were handed in upon that day, and they have no means of identifying this particular one, or of remembering the sender. The box is a half-pound box of honeydew tobacco and does not help us in any way. The medical student theory still appears to me to be the most feasible, but if you should have a few hours to spare I should be very happy to see you out here. I shall be either at the house or in the police-station all day.

"What say you, Watson? Can you rise superior to the heat and run down to Croydon with me on the off chance of a case for your annals?"

"I was longing for something to do."

"You shall have it then. Ring for our boots and tell them to order a cab. I'll be back in a moment when I have changed my dressing-gown and filled my cigar-case."

A shower of rain fell while we were in the train, and the heat was far less oppressive in Croydon than in town. Holmes had sent on a wire, so that Lestrade, as wiry, as dapper, and as ferret- like as ever, was waiting for us at the station. A walk of five minutes took us to Cross Street, where Miss Cushing resided.

It was a very long street of two-story brick houses, neat and prim, with whitened stone steps and little groups of aproned women gossiping at the doors. Halfway down, Lestrade stopped and tapped at a door, which was opened by a small servant girl. Miss Cushing was sitting in the front room, into which we were ushered. She was a placid-faced woman, with large, gentle eyes, and grizzled hair curving down over her temples on each side. A worked antimacassar lay upon her lap and a basket of coloured silks stood upon a stool beside her.

"They are in the outhouse, those dreadful things," said she as Lestrade entered. "I wish that you would take them away altogether."

"So I shall, Miss Cushing. I only kept them here until my friend, Mr. Holmes, should have seen them in your presence."

"Why in my presence, sir?"

"In case he wished to ask any questions."

"What is the use of asking me questions when I tell you I know nothing whatever about it?"

"Quite so, madam," said Holmes in his soothing way. "I have no doubt that you have been annoyed more than enough already over this business."

"Indeed I have, sir. I am a quiet woman and live a retired life. It is something new for me to see my name in the papers and to find the police in my house. I won't have those things I here, Mr. Lestrade. If you wish to see them you must go to the outhouse."

It was a small shed in the narrow garden which ran behind the house. Lestrade went in and brought out a yellow cardboard box, with a piece of brown paper and some string. There was a bench at the end of the path, and we all sat down while Homes examined one by one, the articles which Lestrade had handed to him.

"The string is exceedingly interesting," he remarked, holding it up to the light and sniffing at it. "What do you make of this string, Lestrade?"

"It has been tarred."

"Precisely. It is a piece of tarred twine. You have also, no doubt, remarked that Miss Cushing has cut the cord with a scissors, as can be seen by the double fray on each side. This is of importance."

"I cannot see the importance," said Lestrade.

"The importance lies in the fact that the knot is left intact, and that this knot is of a peculiar character."

"It is very neatly tied. I had already made a note of that effect," said Lestrade complacently.

"So much for the string, then," said Holmes, smiling, "now for the box wrapper. Brown paper, with a distinct smell of coffee. What, did you not observe it? I think there can be no doubt of it. Address printed in rather straggling characters: 'Miss S. Cushing, Cross Street, Croydon.' Done with a broad-pointed pen, probably a J, and with very inferior ink. The word 'Croydon' has been originally spelled with an 'i', which has been changed to 'y'. The parcel was directed, then, by a man—the printing is distinctly masculine—of limited education and unacquainted with the town of Croydon. So far, so good! The box is a yellow, half-pound honeydew box, with nothing distinctive save two thumb marks at the left bottom corner. It is filled with rough salt of the quality used for preserving hides and other of the coarser commercial purposes. And embedded in it are these very singular enclosures."

He took out the two ears as he spoke, and laying a board across his knee he examined them minutely, while Lestrade and I, bending forward on each side of him, glanced alternately at these dreadful relics and at the thoughtful, eager face of our companion. Finally he returned them to the box once more and sat for a while in deep meditation.

"You have observed, of course," said he at last, "that the ears are not a pair."

"Yes, I have noticed that. But if this were the practical joke of some students from the dissecting-rooms, it would be as easy for them to send two odd ears as a pair."

"Precisely. But this is not a practical joke."

"You are sure of it?"

"The presumption is strongly against it. Bodies in the dissecting-rooms are injected with preservative fluid. These ears bear no signs of this. They are fresh, too. They have been cut off with a blunt instrument, which would hardly happen if a student had done it. Again, carbolic or rectified spirits would be the preservatives which would suggest themselves to the medical mind, certainly not rough salt. I repeat that there is no practical joke here, but that we are investigating a serious crime."

A vague thrill ran through me as I listened to my companion's words and saw the stern gravity which had hardened his features. This brutal preliminary seemed to shadow forth some strange and inexplicable horror in the background. Lestrade, however, shook his head like a man who is only half convinced.

"There are objections to the joke theory, no doubt," said he, "but there are much stronger reasons against the other. We know that this woman has led a most quiet and respectable life at Penge and here for the last twenty years. She has hardly been away from her home for a day during that time. Why on earth, then, should any criminal send her the proofs of his guilt, especially as, unless she is a most consummate actress, she understands quite as little of the matter as we do?"

"That is the problem which we have to solve," Holmes answered, "and for my part I shall set about it by presuming that my reasoning is correct, and that a double murder has been committed. One of these ears is a woman's, small, finely formed, and pierced for an earring. The other is a man's, sun-burned, discoloured, and also pierced for an earring. These two people are presumably dead, or we should have heard their story before now. To-day is Friday. The packet was posted on Thursday morning. The tragedy, then, occurred on Wednesday or Tuesday, or earlier. If the two people were murdered, who but their murderer would have sent this sign of his work to Miss Cushing? We may take it that the sender of the packet is the man whom we want. But he must have some strong reason for sending Miss Cushing this packet. What reason then? It must have been to tell her that the deed was done! or to pain her, perhaps. But in that case she knows who it is. Does she know? I doubt it. If she knew, why should she call the police in? She might have buried the ears, and no one would have been the wiser. That is what she would have done if she had wished to shield the criminal. But if she does not wish to shield him she would give his name. There is a tangle here which needs straightening to." He had been talking in a high, quick voice, staring blankly up over the garden fence, but now he sprang briskly to his feet and walked towards the house.

"I have a few questions to ask Miss Cushing," said he.

"In that case I may leave you here," said Lestrade, "for I have another small business on hand. I think that I have nothing further to learn form Miss Cushing. You will find me at the police-station."

"We shall look in on our way to the train," answered Holmes. A moment later he and I were back in the front room, where the impassive lady was still quietly working away at her antimacassar. She put it down on her lap as we entered and looked at us with her frank, searching blue eyes.

"I am convinced, sir," she said, "that this matter is a mistake, and that the parcel was never meant for me at all. I have said this several times to the gentlemen from Scotland Yard, but he simply laughs at me. I have not an enemy in the world, as far as I know, so why should anyone play me such a trick?"

"I am coming to be of the same opinion, Miss Cushing," said Holmes, taking a seat beside her. "I think that it is more than probable—" He paused, and I was surprised, on glancing round to see that he was staring with singular intentness at the lady's profile. Surprise and satisfaction were both for an instant to be read upon his eager face, though when she glanced round to find out the cause of his silence he had become as demure as ever. I stared hard myself at her flat, grizzled hair, her trim cap, her little gilt earrings, her placid features; but I could see nothing which could account for my companion's evident excitement.

"There were one or two questions—"

"Oh, I am weary of questions!" cried Miss Cushing impatiently.

"You have two sisters, I believe."

"How could you know that?"

"I observed the very instant that I entered the room that you have a portrait group of three ladies upon the mantelpiece, one of whom is undoubtedly yourself, while the others are so exceedingly like you that there could be no doubt of the relationship."

"Yes, you are quite right. Those are my sisters, Sarah and Mary."

"And here at my elbow is another portrait, taken at Liverpool, of your younger sister, in the company of a man who appears to be a steward by his uniform. I observe that she was unmarried at the time."

"You are very quick at observing."

"That is my trade."

"Well, you are quite right. But she was married to Mr. Browner a few days afterwards. He was on the South American line when that was taken, but he was so fond of her that he couldn't abide to leave her for so long, and he got into the Liverpool and London boats."

"Ah, the Conqueror, perhaps?"

"No, the May Day, when last I heard. Jim came down here to see me once. That was before he broke the pledge; but afterwards he would always take drink when he was ashore, and a little drink would send him stark, staring mad. Ah! it was a bad day that ever he took a glass in his hand again. First he dropped me, then he quarrelled with Sarah, and now that Mary has stopped writing we don't know how things are going with them."

It was evident that Miss Cushing had come upon a subject on which she felt very deeply. Like most people who lead a lonely life, she was shy at first, but ended by becoming extremely communicative. She told us many details about her brother-in-law the steward, and then wandering off on the subject of her former lodgers, the medical students, she gave us a long account of their delinquencies, with their names and those of their hospitals. Holmes listened attentively to everything, throwing in a question from time to time.

"About your second sister, Sarah," said he. "I wonder, since you are both maiden ladies, that you do not keep house together."

"Ah! you don't know Sarah's temper or you would wonder no more. I tried it when I came to Croydon, and we kept on until about two months ago, when we had to part. I don't want to say a word against my own sister, but she was always meddlesome and hard to please, was Sarah."

"You say that she quarrelled with your Liverpool relations."

"Yes, and they were the best of friends at one time. Why, she went up there to live in order to be near them. And now she has no word hard enough for Jim Browner. The last six months that she was here she would speak of nothing but his drinking and his ways. He had caught her meddling, I suspect, and given her a bit of his mind, and that was the start of it."

"Thank you, Miss Cushing," said Holmes, rising and bowing. "Your sister Sarah lives, I think you said, at New Street, Wallington? Good-bye, and I am very sorry that you should have been troubled over a case with which, as you say, you have nothing whatever to do."

There was a cab passing as we came out, and Holmes hailed it.

"How far to Wallington?" he asked.

"Only about a mile, sir."

"Very good. Jump in, Watson. We must strike while the iron is hot. Simple as the case is, there have been one or two very instructive details in connection with it. Just pull up at a telegraph office as you pass, cabby."

Holmes sent off a short wire and for the rest of the drive lay back in the cab, with his hat tilted over his nose to keep the sun from his face. Our drive pulled up at a house which was not unlike the one which we had just quitted. My companion ordered him to wait, and had his hand upon the knocker, when the door opened and a grave young gentleman in black, with a very shiny hat, appeared on the step.

"Is Miss Cushing at home?" asked Holmes.

"Miss Sarah Cushing is extremely ill," said he. "She has been suffering since yesterday from brain symptoms of great severity. As her medical adviser, I cannot possibly take the responsibility of allowing anyone to see her. I should recommend you to call again in ten days." He drew on his gloves, closed the door, and marched off down the street.

"Well, if we can't we can't," said Holmes, cheerfully.

"Perhaps she could not or would not have told you much."

"I did not wish her to tell me anything. I only wanted to look at her. However, I think that I have got all that I want. Drive us to some decent hotel, cabby, where we may have some lunch, and afterwards we shall drop down upon friend Lestrade at the police- station."

We had a pleasant little meal together, during which Holmes would talk about nothing but violins, narrating with great exultation how he had purchased his own Stradivarius, which was worth at least five hundred guineas, at a Jew broker's in Tottenham Court Road for fifty-five shillings. This led him to Paganini, and we sat for an hour over a bottle of claret while he told me anecdote after anecdote of that extraordinary man. The afternoon was far advanced and the hot glare had softened into a mellow glow before we found ourselves at the police-station. Lestrade was waiting for us at the door.

"A telegram for you, Mr. Holmes," said he.

"Ha! It is the answer!" He tore it open, glanced his eyes over it, and crumpled it into his pocket. "That's all right," said he.

"Have you found out anything?"

"I have found out everything!"

"What!" Lestrade stared at him in amazement. "You are joking."

"I was never more serious in my life. A shocking crime has been committed, and I think I have now laid bare every detail of it."

"And the criminal?"

Holmes scribbled a few words upon the back of one of his visiting cards and threw it over to Lestrade.

"That is the name," he said. "You cannot effect an arrest until to-morrow night at the earliest. I should prefer that you do not mention my name at all in connection with the case, as I choose to be only associated with those crimes which present some difficulty in their solution. Come on, Watson." We strode off together to the station, leaving Lestrade still staring with a delighted face at the card which Holmes had thrown him.

"The case," said Sherlock Holmes as we chatted over or cigars that night in our rooms at Baker Street, "is one where, as in the investigations which you have chronicled under the names of 'A Study in Scarlet' and of 'The Sign of Four,' we have been compelled to reason backward from effects to causes. I have written to Lestrade asking him to supply us with the details which are now wanting, and which he will only get after he had secured his man. That he may be safely trusted to do, for although he is absolutely devoid of reason, he is as tenacious as a bulldog when he once understands what he has to do, and indeed, it is just this tenacity which has brought him to the top at Scotland Yard."

"Your case is not complete, then?" I asked.

"It is fairly complete in essentials. We know who the author of the revolting business is, although one of the victims still escapes us. Of course, you have formed your own conclusions."

"I presume that this Jim Browner, the steward of a Liverpool boat, is the man whom you suspect?"

"Oh! it is more than a suspicion."

"And yet I cannot see anything save very vague indications."

"On the contrary, to my mind nothing could be more clear. Let me run over the principal steps. We approached the case, you remember, with an absolutely blank mind, which is always an advantage. We had formed no theories. We were simply there to observe and to draw inferences from our observations. What did we see first? A very placid and respectable lady, who seemed quite innocent of any secret, and a portrait which showed me that she had two younger sisters. It instantly flashed across my mind that the box might have been meant for one of these. I set the idea aside as one which could be disproved or confirmed at our leisure. Then we went to the garden, as you remember, and we saw the very singular contents of the little yellow box.

"The string was of the quality which is used by sail-makers aboard ship, and at once a whiff of the sea was perceptible in our investigation. When I observed that the knot was one which is popular with sailors, that the parcel had been posted at a port, and that the male ear was pierced for an earring which is so much more common among sailors than landsmen, I was quite certain that all the actors in the tragedy were to be found among our seafaring classes.

"When I came to examine the address of the packet I observed that it was to Miss S. Cushing. Now, the oldest sister would, of course, be Miss Cushing, and although her initial was 'S' it might belong to one of the others as well. In that case we should have to commence our investigation from a fresh basis altogether. I therefore went into the house with the intention of clearing up this point. I was about to assure Miss Cushing that I was convinced that a mistake had been made when you may remember that I came suddenly to a stop. The fact was that I had just seen something which filled me with surprise and at the same time narrowed the field of our inquiry immensely.

"As a medical man, you are aware, Watson, that there is no part of the body which varies so much as the human ear. Each ear is as a rule quite distinctive and differs from all other ones. In last year's Anthropological Journal you will find two short monographs from my pen upon the subject. I had, therefore, examined the ears in the box with the eyes of an expert and had carefully noted their anatomical peculiarities. Imagine my surprise, then, when on looking at Miss Cushing I perceived that her ear corresponded exactly with the female ear which I had just inspected. The matter was entirely beyond coincidence. There was the same shortening of the pinna, the same broad curve of the upper lobe, the same convolution of the inner cartilage. In all essentials it was the same ear.

"In the first place, her sister's name was Sarah, and her address had until recently been the same, so that it was quite obvious how the mistake had occurred and for whom the packet was meant. Then we heard of this steward, married to the third sister, and learned that he had at one time been so intimate with Miss Sarah that she had actually gone up to Liverpool to be near the Browners, but a quarrel had afterwards divided them. This quarrel had put a stop to all communications for some months, so that if Browner had occasion to address a packet to Miss Sarah, he would undoubtedly have done so to her old address.

"And now the matter had begun to straighten itself out wonderfully. We had learned of the existence of this steward, an impulsive man, of strong passions—you remember that he threw up what must have been a very superior berth in order to be nearer to his wife—subject, too, to occasional fits of hard drinking. We had reason to believe that his wife had been murdered, and that a man— presumably a seafaring man—had been murdered at the same time. Jealousy, of course, at once suggests itself as the motive for the crime. And why should these proofs of the deed be sent to Miss Sarah Cushing? Probably because during her residence in Liverpool she had some hand in bringing about the events which led to the tragedy. You will observe that this line of boats call at Belfast, Dublin, and Waterford; so that, presuming that Browner had committed the deed and had embarked at once upon his steamer, the May Day, Belfast would be the first place at which he cold post his terrible packet.

"A second solution was at this stage obviously possible, and although I thought it exceedingly unlikely, I was determined to elucidate it before going further. An unsuccessful lover might have killed Mr. and Mrs. Browner, and the male ear might have belonged to the husband. There were many grave objections to this theory, but it was conceivable. I therefore sent off a telegram to my friend Algar, of the Liverpool force, and asked him to find our if Mrs. Browner were at home, and if Browner had departed in the May Day. Then we went on to Wallington to visit Miss Sarah.

"I was curious, in the first place, to see how far the family ear had been reproduced in her. Then, of course, she might give us very important information, but I was not sanguine that she would. She must have heard of the business the day before, since all Croydon was ringing with it, and she alone could have understood for whom the packet was meant. If she had been willing to help justice she would probably have communicated with the police already. However, it was clearly our duty to see her, so we went. We found that the news of the arrival of the packet- - for her illness dated from that time—had such an effect upon her as to bring on brain fever. It was clearer than ever that she understood its full significance, but equally clear that we should have to wait some time for any assistance from her.

"However, we were really independent of her help. Our answers were waiting for us at the police-station, where I had directed Algar to send them. Nothing could be more conclusive. Mrs. Browner's house had been closed for more than three days, and the neighbours were of opinion that she had gone south to see her relatives. It had been ascertained at the shipping offices that Browner had left aboard of the May Day, and I calculate that she is due in the Thames tomorrow night. When he arrives he will be met by the obtuse but resolute Lestrade, and I have no doubt that we shall have all our details filled in."

Sherlock Holmes was not disappointed in his expectations. Two days later he received a bulky envelope, which contained a short note from the detective, and a typewritten document, which covered several pages of foolscap.

"Lestrade has got him all right," said Holmes, glancing up at me. "Perhaps it would interest you to hear what he says.

"My dear Mr. Holmes:

In accordance with the scheme which we had formed in order to test our theories" ["the 'we' is rather fine, Watson, is it not?"] "I went down to the Albert Dock yesterday at 6 p.m., and boarded the S.S. May Day, belonging to the Liverpool, Dublin, and London Steam Packet Company. On inquiry, I found that there was a steward on board of the name of James Browner and that he had acted during the voyage in such an extraordinary manner that the captain had been compelled to relieve him of his duties. On descending to his berth, I found him seated upon a chest with his head sunk upon his hands, rocking himself to and fro. He is a big, powerful chap, clean-shaven, and very swarthy—something like Aldrige, who helped us in the bogus laundry affair. He jumped up when he heard my business, and I had my whistle to my lips to call a couple of river police, who were round the corner, but he seemed to have no heart in him, and he held out his hands quietly enough for the darbies. We brought him along to the cells, and his box as well, for we thought there might be something incriminating; but, bar a big sharp knife such as most sailors have, we got nothing for our trouble. However, we find that we shall want no more evidence, for on being brought before the inspector at the station he asked leave to make a statement, which was, of course, taken down, just as he made it, by our shorthand man. We had three copies typewritten, one of which I enclose. The affair proves, as I always thought it would, to be an extremely simple one, but I am obliged to you for assisting me in my investigation. With kind regards,

"Yours very truly,

"G. Lestrade.

"Hum! The investigation really was a very simple one," remarked Holmes, "but I don't think it struck him in that light when he first called us in. However, let us see what Jim Browner has to say for himself. This is his statement as made before Inspector Montgomery at the Shadwell Police Station, and it has the advantage of being verbatim."

"'Have I anything to say? Yes, I have a deal to say. I have to make a clean breast of it all. You can hang me, or you can leave me alone. I don't care a plug which you do. I tell you I've not shut an eye in sleep since I did it, and I don't believe I ever will again until I get past all waking. Sometimes it's his face, but most generally it's hers. I'm never without one or the other before me. He looks frowning and black-like, but she has a kind o' surprise upon her face. Ay, the white lamb, she might well be surprised when she read death on a face that had seldom looked anything but love upon her before.

"'But it was Sarah's fault, and may the curse of a broken man put a blight on her and set the blood rotting in her veins! It's not that I want to clear myself. I know that I went back to drink, like the beast that I was. But she would have forgiven me; she would have stuck as close to me a rope to a block if that woman had never darkened our door. For Sarah Cushing loved me—that's the root of the business—she loved me until all her love turned to poisonous hate when she knew that I thought more of my wife's footmark in the mud than I did of her whole body and soul.

"'There were three sisters altogether. The old one was just a good woman, the second was a devil, and the third was an angel. Sarah was thirty-three, and Mary was twenty-nine when I married. We were just as happy as the day was long when we set up house together, and in all Liverpool there was no better woman than my Mary. And then we asked Sarah up for a week, and the week grew into a month, and one thing led to another, until she was just one of ourselves.

"'I was blue ribbon at that time, and we were putting a little money by, and all was as bright as a new dollar. My God, whoever would have thought that it cold have come to this? Whoever would have dreamed it?

"'I used to be home for the week-ends very often, and sometimes if the ship were held back for cargo I would have a whole week at a time, and in this way I saw a deal of my sister-in-law, Sarah. She was a fine tall woman, black and quick and fierce, with a proud way of carrying her head, and a glint from her eye like a spark from a flint. But when little Mary was there I had never a thought of her, and that I swear as I hope for God's mercy.

"'It had seemed to me sometimes that she liked to be alone with me, or to coax me out for a walk with her, but I had never thought anything of that. But one evening my eyes were opened. I had come up from the ship and found my wife out, but Sarah at home. "Where's Mary?" I asked. "Oh, she has gone to pay some accounts." I was impatient and paced up and down the room. "Can't you be happy for five minutes without Mary, Jim?" says she. "It's a bad compliment to me that you can't be contented with my society for so short a time." "That's all right, my lass," said I, putting out my hand towards her in a kindly way, but she had it in both hers in an instant, and they burned as if they were in a fever. I looked into her eyes and I read it all there. There was no need for her to speak, nor for me either. I frowned and drew my hand away. Then she stood by my side in silence for a bit, and then put up her hand and patted me on the shoulder. "Steady old Jim!" said she, and with a kind o' mocking laugh, she ran out of the room.

"'Well, from that time Sarah hated me with her whole heart and soul, and she is a woman who can hate, too. I was a fool to let her go on biding with us—a besotted fool—but I never said a word to Mary, for I knew it would grieve her. Things went on much as before, but after a time I began to find that there was a bit of a change in Mary herself. She had always been so trusting and so innocent, but now she became queer and suspicious, wanting to know where I had been and what I had been doing, and whom my letters were from, and what I had in my pockets, and a thousand such follies. Day by day she grew queerer and more irritable, and we had ceaseless rows about nothing. I was fairly puzzled by it all. Sarah avoided me now, but she and Mary were just inseparable. I can see now how she was plotting and scheming and poisoning my wife's mind against me, but I was such a blind beetle that I could not understand it at the time. Then I broke my blue ribbon and began to drink again, but I think I should not have done it if Mary had been the same as ever. She had some reason to be disgusted with me now, and the gap between us began to be wider and wider. And then this Alec Fairbairn chipped in, and things became a thousand times blacker.

"'It was to see Sarah that he came to my house first, but soon it was to see us, for he was a man with winning ways, and he made friends wherever he went. He was a dashing, swaggering chap, smart and curled, who had seen half the world and could talk of what he had seen. He was good company, I won't deny it, and he had wonderful polite ways with him for a sailor man, so that I think there must have been a time when he knew more of the poop than the forecastle. For a month he was in and out of my house, and never once did it cross my mind that harm might come of his soft, tricky ways. And then at last something made me suspect, and from that day my peace was gone forever.

"'It was only a little thing, too. I had come into the parlour unexpected, and as I walked in at the door I saw a light of welcome on my wife's face. But as she saw who it was it faded again, and she turned away with a look of disappointment. That was enough for me. There was no one but Alec Fairbairn whose step she could have mistaken for mine. If I could have seen him then I should have killed him, for I have always been like a madman when my temper gets loose. Mary saw the devil's light in my eyes, and she ran forward with her hands on my sleeve. "Don't, Jim, don't!" says she. "Where's Sarah?" I asked. "In the kitchen," says she. "Sarah," says I as I went in, "this man

Fairbairn is never to darken my door again." "Why not?" says she. "Because I order it." "Oh!" says she, "if my friends are not good enough for this house, then I am not good enough for it either." "You can do what you like," says I, "but if Fairbairn shows his face here again I'll send you one of his ears for a keepsake." She was frightened by my face, I think, for she never answered a word, and the same evening she left my house.

"'Well, I don't know now whether it was pure devilry on the part of this woman, or whether she thought that she could turn me against my wife by encouraging her to misbehave. Anyway, she took a house just two streets off and let lodgings to sailors. Fairbairn used to stay there, and Mary would go round to have tea with her sister and him. How often she went I don't know, but I followed her one day, and as I broke in at the door Fairbairn got away over the back garden wall, like the cowardly skunk that he was. I swore to my wife that I would kill her if I found her in his company again, and I led her back with me, sobbing and trembling, and as white as a piece of paper. There was no trace of love between us any longer. I could see that she hated me and feared me, and when the thought of it drove me to drink, then she despised me as well.

"'Well, Sarah found that she could not make a living in Liverpool, so she went back, as I understand, to live with her sister in Croydon, and things jogged on much the same as ever at home. And then came this week and all the misery and ruin.

"'It was in this way. We had gone on the May Day for a round voyage of seven days, but a hogshead got loose and started one of our plates, so that we had to put back into port for twelve hours. I left the ship and came home, thinking what a surprise it would be for my wife, and hoping that maybe she would be glad to see me so soon. The thought was in my head as I turned into my own street, and at that moment a cab passed me, and there she was, sitting by the side of Fairbairn, the two chatting and laughing, with never a thought for me as I stood watching them from the footpath.

"'I tell you, and I give you my word for it, that from that moment I was not my own master, and it is all like a dim dream when I look back on it. I had been drinking hard of late, and the two things together fairly turned my brain. There's something throbbing in my head now, like a docker's hammer, but that morning I seemed to have all Niagara whizzing and buzzing in my ears.

"'Well, I took to my heels, and I ran after the cab. I had a heavy oak stick in my hand, and I tell you I saw red from the first; but as I ran I got cunning, too, and hung back a little to see them without being seen. They pulled up soon at the railway station. There was a good crowd round the booking-office, so I got quite close to them without being seen. They took tickets for New Brighton. So did I, but I got in three carriages behind them. When we reached it they walked along the Parade, and I was never more than a hundred yards from them. At last I saw them hire a boat and start for a row, for it was a very hot day, and they thought, no doubt, that it would be cooler on the water.

"'It was just as if they had been given into my hands. There was a bit of a haze, and you could not see more than a few hundred yards. I hired a boat for myself, and I pulled after them. I could see the blur of their craft, but they were going nearly as fast as I, and they must have been a long mile from the shore before I caught them up. The haze was like a curtain all round us, and there were we three in the middle of it. My God, shall I ever forget their faces when they saw who was in the boat that was closing in upon them? She screamed out. He swore like a madman and jabbed at me with an oar, for he must have seen death in my eyes. I got past it and got one in with my stick that crushed his head like an egg. I would have spared her, perhaps, for all my madness, but she threw her arms round him, crying out to him, and calling him "Alec." I struck again, and she lay stretched beside him. I was like a wild beast then that had tasted blood. If Sarah had been there, by the Lord, she should have joined them. I pulled out my knife, and—well, there! I've said enough. It gave me a kind of savage joy when I thought how Sarah would feel when she had such signs as these of what her meddling had brought about. Then I tied the bodies into the boat, stove a plank, and stood by until they had sunk. I knew very well that the owner would think that they had lost their bearings in the haze, and had drifted off out to sea. I cleaned myself up, got back to land, and joined my ship without a soul having a suspicion of what had passed. That night I made up the packet for Sarah Cushing, and next day I sent it from Belfast.

"'There you have the whole truth of it. You can hang me, or do what you like with me, but you cannot punish me as I have been punished already. I cannot shut my eyes but I see those two faces staring at me—staring at me as they stared when my boat broke through the haze. I killed them quick, but they are killing me slow; and if I have another night of it I shall be either mad or dead before morning. You won't put me alone into a cell, sir? For pity's sake don't, and may you be treated in your day of agony as you treat me now.'

"What is the meaning of it, Watson?" said Holmes solemnly as he laid down the paper. "What object is served by this circle of misery and violence and fear? It must tend to some end, or else our universe is ruled by chance, which is unthinkable. But what end? There is the great standing perennial problem to which human reason is as far from an answer as ever.

Made in United States
North Haven, CT
03 July 2022